Wellsprings

A Fable of Consciousness

Wellsprings

A Fable of Consciousness

William T. Hathaway

COSMIC
EGG
BOOKS

Winchester, UK
Washington, USA

First published by Cosmic Egg Books, 2013
Cosmic Egg Books is an imprint of John Hunt Publishing Ltd., Laurel House, Station Approach,
Alresford, Hants, SO24 9JH, UK
office1@jhpbooks.net
www.johnhuntpublishing.com

For distributor details and how to order please visit the 'Ordering' section on our website.

ISBN: 978 1 78099 994 4

A CIP catalogue record for this book is available from the British Library.

Design: Stuart Davies

Printed in the USA by Edwards Brothers Malloy

We operate a distinctive and ethical publishing philosophy in all
areas of our business, from our global network of authors to
production and worldwide distribution.

For Maharishi Mahesh Yogi

The author would like to thank Daniela Rommel, Bob Schuster, Stephen Weichman, Michael Shickich, and Ken Chawkin.

Pack my rucksack and get out of this place. Like the song says, "I'm leavin' LA, baby. Don't you know this smog has got me down." Taj Mahal. I found his album—one of those old black discs—in a box with a bunch of others in granddad's garage. Old record player with it, kind that goes around and 'round. Been listening to them ever since—all gramp's favorites from the sixties and seventies when he was a kid. Great songs...scratches and all.

He said the smog then was nothing compared to what we got now. They didn't have alkali smog back then. We're breathing borax and potash blown in with the dust. Granddad died of emphysema but he never smoked. The doc said some people are more sensitive than others. I got his heredity. Mom and dad coughing, especially when they wake up. Even hear the neighbors coughing. Gotta get outa here. "We gotta get out of this place, if it's the last thing we ever do." Another song—The Animals.

Animals now are dying even in the zoos. Birds gone.

Like to take all his old records with me, but no room in the rucksack. They'll be here when I come back...if I come back. Mom and dad will be pissed I just left them a letter. But if I told them, they'd just pressure me into staying again, like they did last time I told them I wanted to go. No money for college. They want me to get some shit job here. If I'm going to have a shit job, I want it to be at least some place where I can breathe.

Rucksack's pretty heavy. Outta here.

Little bungalow house like all the others. Dust on the windowsills. Sand in the drain spouts. Hasn't rained this year.

Wind patterns changed so it rains over the ocean but hardly ever over the land. Grass died, then even the weeds died. At least the dirt won't die. The Great Drought, they call it. I don't know what's so great about it.

Strap the pack on the back of the little Honda 250 bike, spark it alive. So long, Long Beach. Miles of bungalows, fourplex apartments, gas stations, strip malls. Sand on the road, sand in the gutters, sky cloudless but gray. Plenty of water for people who can afford it, but there's fewer and fewer of those. Outta here.

Onto the Golden State Freeway—what a joke. All the gold belongs to the people in the big houses behind gates with green lawns and swimming pools. Beverly Hills, Palos Verdes, San Marino—oases in the desert. Water for the rest of us is rationed, but they buy all they want from the private companies—pay a fortune. But they've got a fortune, so it's no problem.

North. Cooler there...maybe they still have dew. Never seen dew. Must be wonderful. Want to see Yosemite. Maybe I can get a job there. I better. $320 won't last long.

Cars filthy, people can't afford to wash them. Some of the people filthy too.

Stop in Santa Clarita for gas. Wash up first—face grimy, eyes stinging despite the visor, cough up brown crud. Rinse off my helmet and windbreaker.

Pump the gas. Big tanker truck with a trailer pulls into the other slot. Guy gets out—heavy set, round face, almost bald but a thick salt-and-pepper mustache, camo T-shirt, khaki pants, running shoes. Smiles and says, "Wish this truck got your gas mileage."

I point to my face and say, "Wish this bike had your windshield."

"Yeah, well, that's life. It's always something." He lights a cigarette despite the sign. "Where you headed?"

"North."

"Me too. You want a job?"

2

Why would he ask someone he doesn't even know? "What doing?" I ask warily.

"Roustabout, general labor, simple mechanical stuff you can learn. We're drilling and pumping water. We can put your bike in the back. You won't have to drive."

"Why me?"

"Guy I had just left me in the lurch. You look strong enough to do the job. I can't afford to pay much, so it's hard to find help."

"What does it pay?"

"Fifty bucks a day."

"You're drilling for water? I thought all the wells were dry...water table's gone."

"Mostly that's true. But there's still some places that got water. A few underground springs here and there. The trick is knowing where to drill."

"You travel around, looking for water?" I ask him.

"Yeah. You from LA?"

"Yeah."

"You'll get to see the rest of California," he says.

"How often would I get paid?"

"That sounds like you just want to make a few bucks and split. That I don't need again."

I don't get a bad feeling from the guy, and I need the money. If it turns out there's a hitch, I'll quit."How about if I try it for a week. As long as everything's OK, I'll stick with it."

"Fair enough. Then you get paid every week. Cash. No taxes."

"But that probably means no benefits. No unemployment or medical."

"That's the way it is now. New economy. Every man for himself. I got those pressures too. We're both in the same boat." He shrugs. "That's the best I can offer."

"I'll give it a try." We shake on it. He has a real firm grip, so I squeeze back.

"We'll put your bike in the trailer." He opens the tarp

covering the ten-foot trailer and lowers the gate at the end while I wheel the bike around. In the bed lie lengths of plastic pipe, a big metal contraption, and a gas motor. He pushes the pipes aside to make room for the bike, and we heft it in, rucksack and all. Pointing to the contraption, he says, "This is a Big Beaver drill rig. A real honey. We can sink a well down to 250 feet with it. I'll teach you all about it."

We walk to the cab, and he opens the door and says to someone inside, "We got a new roustabout."

A woman leans out, sees me, and smiles. "Welcome aboard." Tan skin, long black hair braided into a single strand down her back. White blouse well filled out and embroidered with red flowers. Silver crucifix around her neck.

"This is my wife, Cora," the man says. "And what's your name?"

"Bob Parks."

"I'm Gene, Gene Reynolds."

I shake hands with Cora, and she smiles again. Red lips, broad high cheekbones. "Get on in," she says and scoots over on the seat. From the sun visor on her side dangles a small teddy bear, from his a .50-caliber machine gun cartridge. On the dashboard jiggles a hula dancer. Two half-empty giant cups of Pepsi Light sit in the drink holder.

I like riding in a big truck. Maybe he'll let me drive it someday. Sitting way up above the road, the opposite of a bike where it's whizzing by right under you. Both are better than a car, where you're just sort of in the middle.

"We're headed for Owens Lake," Gene says, rumbling out onto the freeway. "It's not a lake anymore, just dry mud, but there's a spring that's still active. We got a bore hole drilled there, going to pump it out. We're water wildcatters. Ever hear of those?"

"No."

"You are a city boy, aren't you? We're like the old prospectors,

4

but instead of gold, we're after water. Cora here," he raises his elbow towards his wife, "has the gift of water witching." Cora smiles."She can tell where underground streams are."

"Not by myself I can't tell," Cora corrects him, "but with a willow branch. I hold it in my hands and can feel what it's saying, where the water is. Willows are tuned in to water—they need lots of it. And I can tune in to the willow. The thing is, the branch needs to be fresh, and willows are hard to find now...'cause there's not enough water. Vicious cycle. We got a couple of trees at home. We take real good care of them, so they don't mind sparing me a branch every now and then."

"Where's home?" I ask.

"Simi Valley," Cora says. Her Spanish accent gives her speech lilting rhythms, sharp consonants, and clear vowels.

"But we stay on the move," Gene adds. "Only way to make a living in this biz. We got a bunch of bore holes, and we make the rounds and pump them out. It takes about two weeks for them to fill up again. We got a regular route. But after a while they run dry, so we're always prospecting for new sites to drill. It's a tough way to make a living, but everything's tough these days. I used to be a building contractor, but no one's building now."

The road starts rising through the San Gabriel Mountains, arid rocky heaps dotted with dead tree trunks. "When I first came here," Cora says, "this was a pine forest. We used to drive here on the weekends—cool and shady, and you could wade in the streams. Now the streams are gone. Only things that can grow here is mesquite, sage brush, yucca."

Over the pass, we drop down into the Mojave Desert, where the sparse vegetation of the mountains yields to barren, baked earth. "Why look for water here?" I ask.

"Less competition. There's not so many water wildcatters here as over in the Central Valley," Gene says. "There it's a madhouse. Farmers are desperate for water, drilling and pumping wherever they can. Lots of cops to bust you. Over here there's fewer aquifers, but they haven't all been pumped out, still got some water in 'em. But you gotta go deep."

"This too didn't use to be so dry," Cora says. "It's high desert and had lots of chaparral like the mountains have now. Scrub oak, even grass. They used to graze cattle and sheep here. Now all that's gone."

Gene gestures out the window. "What you see over there, looks like a riverbed? That's the LA Aqueduct, still got a trickle of water in it. There's definitely water here. Trick is to find it. That's our job. Cora's job, really. She's good at it. My job is to drill and pump it out. That's your job too now.

"This spring where we're headed is a small one. We'll probably get just one tanker load out of it, sell it to the Lone Pine Indian Reservation. It's not good for drinking, but it's fine for crops, and a lot cheaper than they can get from the county water department.

"Then we've got a couple of springs up in the Sierra foothills. They get what little runoff still comes down from the mountains. That's better quality water and more of it. We'll sell that to a private water company in Bishop. On the way we'll prospect for more sites and hopefully drill a couple."

Gene and Cora seem all right. Down-home, not phony.

Hours later we pull off onto a dirt road and stop. Ahead of us stretch miles of cracked, curling mud rimmed with white alkali. Bare mountains rise to the west. The only sign of people is a motor home parked off to the side.

"All that mud used to be a lake," Gene says. "LA drank it dry about fifty years ago, but then about twenty-five years ago, 'round the turn of the century, they started restoring it, letting more water in, which meant less for LA. Environmentalists forced them to do it, through the courts. But now with the big drought, water's stopped running into it. Only one spring left."

Gene opens his door, and I open mine but regret it as soon as I do. The cab is air-conditioned, so the air outside seems superheated. I don't even want to breathe, it's so hot. The only water I can see is a round pool with concrete sides, like a small swimming pool but smelling of sulfur. "This is the water?" I ask Gene.

"Not our water," he says. "Our bore hole is over there." He and Cora walk towards a pile of rocks, and I follow. They clear the rocks away to reveal a six-inch wide plastic pipe sunk into the ground. "We went down almost 250 feet to get past the sulfur. The water's still not great, but it's a lot better than that. This used to be a hot springs...been closed for years, though."

Gene looks around, then his face brightens. "Hey, a barrel cactus!" He points to it, a spiny green mound like a miniature fire hydrant. "They're good. Get the machete, Cora."

She goes to the truck and comes back with a big knife. Gene lops the cactus off at the ground and hacks it into three parts. "They call these desert watermelons," he says. "Grab one. Just be careful where you grab." He picks up a piece and begins to chew. "Good!"

I try one. The moist pulp is refreshing in the heat but puckers my mouth. Close to the rind it gets bitter. He shouldn't have killed it.

Gene stares at the motor home. "Wonder how long they're going to stay. I don't like somebody around when we're pumping."

At that moment the door to the motor home opens; a woman steps out and walks towards us. Gene puts his hands on his hips and waits. "Hello," she says with a lift of her hand and a smile. "Welcome, but I want to warn you about the fire ants. If you're going to camp, I'd recommend the other side over there." She's short and thin, wearing light cotton pants, a colorful long-sleeved shirt with buttons but no collar, and a blue sun hat. About mom's age. "They got me pretty good at first. That's why I'm wearing these now." She points to her hiking boots with her pant legs tucked into them, and we glance nervously down at our feet. No ants.

"Thanks for the warning," Cora says. "We'll take your advice."

"Yeah, thanks," Gene says. "You been here long?"

"Just a couple of hours," the woman replies.

"How long you planning on staying?" he asks.

"Not sure," she says with a shrug of her shoulders. "Few days maybe. Depends on how I like it."

Gene frowns and scratches his chin with his thumb.

She waits a moment, then says, "Well, hope you enjoy your stay," and walks back towards the motor home.

"I don't like it," Gene says to Cora.

"She might not even know what we're doing," Cora replies.

Gene lights a cigarette. "Might not, sure. But she might. All it would take would be one call to the cops."

"What's going on?" I ask.

"We don't want to pump while she's around," Gene says. "Could cause trouble."

My neck is getting tense. "What kind of trouble?"

Gene's eyes meet mine, then glance away. "You see, technically we're not supposed to drill and pump water here. The water rights are all bought up by big outfits, and they're trying to squeeze the little guys out. LA Department of Water and Power owns the rights here. Hell, they own all the way up to Reno. They can drill deep enough to get what's left of the water. Their lobby got a law passed to make what we're doing illegal.

"So if she's a law-and-order type and calls 911, the sheriff's going to bust us. The fine would put us out of business. And if we did it again, we'd go to jail."

He looks at me again with wrinkles squinting his eyes. "Don't worry, though. They wouldn't do anything to you. You'd just lose your job. But we'd lose everything. That's why our bore hole is hidden."

I'm getting mad. "You should've told me this before. I didn't know I was getting into something illegal."

Gene shrugs. "I said we were water wildcatters. It's common knowledge that water wildcatting is illegal."

"I didn't know it."

"Well, now you do. But the only reason it's illegal is that the big companies don't want any competition. We're selling water at half their price. For a lot of people, farmers especially, that's all they can afford. We're the last of the entrepreneurs. But this gal may be on the side of the corporations. We gotta find some way to chase her out."

"But she got here first," I say. "She's got a right to stay."

Gene shakes his head in disbelief that I would say anything so dumb. "Attitude like that, you're not going to get very far in this world." He stares up at the pale-blue cloudless sky. "Come on, I got a plan." He walks towards the motor home; Cora and I follow.

The woman is sitting on a folding chair in the shade of her RV reading a book.

"Excuse me," Gene says, and she looks up. "I thought I ought to warn you. We're the advance crew for a biker party. We're going to set the place up, and about a hundred of them are going to be roaring in here tonight. They're a mean bunch, especially when they're drunk. And they're definitely gonna be drunk."

The woman's mouth drops open a bit and her cheeks sink, making her green eyes look larger.

"They got loudspeakers that are gonna be blasting out hard rock all night long."

She closes her eyes in a grimace.

"You seem like a nice lady, and we don't want anything to happen to you...or your motor home. I seen 'em tip one of these things over just for laughs. These guys got a different sense of fun. They get carried away. They won't leave you alone, even if you lock the door...especially if you lock the door."

She swallows with difficulty and says in a small voice, "Oh

my goodness."

Gene touches the tip of his tongue to the bottom edge of his upper teeth, nods his head, and says, "I'd recommend you find a safer place to spend the night."

I look into her eyes, a clear light green, and she looks into mine. Something deep seems to open up inside me. I don't want to see her frightened. I can't be part of Gene's low trick. I turn to him and say, "That's a lie. It's all lies. And I'm not going to let you get away with it." I turn to her and say, "There's no bikers. You can stay as long as you want. He's just trying to scare you." Back to Gene, "I quit!"

"You bastard," he shouts at me, "I'll get you for this!" He stalks back towards the truck; Cora glares at me and follows him.

"Thank you," the woman tells me. "But who is that obstreperous lout?"

I'm not sure what that means.

Gene is opening the rear of the trailer. He drags out my bike and lets it fall to the ground. "Fuck you!" he yells, giving me the finger. He closes the trailer and climbs into the cab of the truck with Cora scurrying after him. They roar away, stirring a cloud of pale dust.

"My bike!" I start towards it.

"Wait," the woman says. "They've already found it."

"Who?"

"Fire ants. Can you see?"

The surface of the bike seems to be moving. "Damn!"

"Is there food in it?"

"In the pack, yeah."

"They must smell it."

"I gotta get it back."

"You can't go just go charging in there. They'll eat you alive. I'll get us some tools." She walks to her Winnebago and returns with a broom and some other stuff.

"You shouldn't have to go over there," I say. "I can do it."

She puts her hands on her hips and stares up at me. "Young man, I've had considerably more experience with fire ants than you have. You could use some help." She hands me some rubber bands. "Put these around your wrists and ankles. Do you have gloves?"

"In the saddle bag."

"Well, I only have one pair, and they're too small for you." She puts on gardening gloves and grips the broom. "You grab the motorcycle, and I'll try to keep them off. We need to move fast. Ready?"

I nod.

"Go!"

I sprint, and as I near the bike, my ankles start stinging. My shoes are covered with ants. I try to stomp them off, but that just makes them madder. The woman is beside me now, flailing with the broom, whooping to me with encouragement then yelping with pain as they attack her too. I try to brush them off my pants, but they cling to my hands, biting with hot jabs. They're bigger, redder, faster, meaner than regular ants.

I grab the handlebars and yank the bike upright. The handlebars are twisted to the side, gas tank dented. The woman brooms it off as I wheel it away.

Some ants have reached my knees on their way up to more sensitive territory. Others are in my shoes, tasting my toes. I can see and feel them on my hands, pincers buried in my meat.

Out of enemy territory near the pool I prop the bike on its kickstand, and she continues to broom it. She notices my hands and says, "Oh dear." She brushes some off with her gloves, but others hold on. She's wincing herself every few seconds from bites.

"Over to the pool," she orders. "Drown the devils."

She sits on the concrete embankment long enough to take off her boots, then hops into the water clothes and all. My clothes and body are crawling with them, my skin afire. I follow her,

11

vaulting over the side, but far enough away not to scare her...although she doesn't seem scared of anything.

She sighs. "Ah, relief!"

My stinging fades by half.

"Sulfur water draws out the venom," she says.

The water doesn't smell or look good, but it feels good—warm and soothing. It's dark and thick, almost slippery, with little things floating in it. Some of those are twigs and strands of algae, but others are ants swimming for the side. They all seem to know the right direction. The sides are concrete covered with greenish black algae. It's a green world here, water a dark blue-green, green iridescent dragon flies hovering and darting, green reeds rimming the pool. Her eyes. There's so little green in the big world now, so it's a luxury to soak in it here. I imagine the pool turning into green amber, and we're floating in it like fossils. Ants too. Someone would find us in a million years and say, "Who were they?"

"Since we're taking a bath together, we should know each other's name," she says.

I laugh. "I'm Bob."

"I'm Jane. Nice to meet you, Bob."

"Thanks for your broom action," I say. "You saved me lots of bites but got lots yourself."

"Glad I could help. A bit of adventure in the day. I appreciate your standing up to those people, not letting them run me off. But why did they want to get rid of me?"

After I explain it to her, she says, "I don't care if they pump water. It's fine with me. I'm no friend of the big companies. Why should the corporations have it all? The rest of us need something in this world. But if he'd lie to me and throw your motorcycle on the ground, I'm glad he's gone. Those sort of people we don't need."

A red-wing blackbird screeches at us from the reeds around the pool. "Must be their nesting time," Jane says. Above us a gull is slicing the air with its scythe-like wings, and higher up a hawk is cruising. A white, long-legged bird struts in the mud nearby. It pauses—one foot raised, head swiveling, round eye scanning—then trots over to a swarm of flies and begins plucking them with its yellow bill.

"Wish that bird would eat some ants," I say.

"They need fish and frogs, things like that. But those aren't here anymore. This used to be a great place for birds—egrets, sandpipers, even pelicans. The water in the lake was shallow, and they could find plenty to eat. Now that the water is gone, they're dying out. That egret is genetically programmed to breed here, but soon they'll all be gone. Just like the trees that used to grow on those hills." She points to the barren gray-brown slopes of the Sierra foothills climbing sharply from the valley floor. "Ponderosa pines don't need much water, but they need some."

"You used to come here?" I ask.

She nods. "Back then it was crowded with campers. There wasn't much water, but some people would paddle kayaks in it. Now this little spring is the only water left. No fire ants back then, just regular picnic ants."

"Speaking of ants, I'd better take care of the bike, check my pack," I say.

"OK. I'm going to soak a bit more. The water is supposed to be good for arthritis."

I clamber out of the pool, scraping off some slimy algae from the side. I'm dripping wet, shoes soaked, but feel better.

No ants on the bike. They must've gone home. I stand it up and wipe it off with a rag from the saddle bag. I use a wrench to loosen the handlebars, then twist them straight again. But I can't fix the dent on the gas tank—popping it out could cause a leak. It doesn't seem to be leaking now, at least. Paint's chipped. Have to live with it this way.

The pack is ripped on the side. I go through it carefully, looking for stragglers, and see with relief they're not in my clothes or sleeping bag. Then I see why: They're all in the food. Most of it's in plastic bags sealed tight enough to keep them out, but they can smell it and are eagerly seeking a way in. I had a chunk of peanut brittle, though, that was just wrapped up. They're all over it, hundreds of them in ant ecstasy. I throw it as far as I can, hoping Jane doesn't mind my littering. I shake and scrape the others off the food bags, getting a few more bites in the process, then pick out some dry clothes and pack everything away.

Jane gets out of the pool and walks to her motor home.

Where should I change? Everything is out in the open. Oh well. I turn my back, wondering if she's watching, then skinny out of my wetties. Red dots like measles on my arms and legs— starting to sting and itch again. I towel off and put the dry clothes on, except for socks. They'd just get soaked from the shoes. I save the dry socks for later and put the wet shoes back on. They're running shoes, so they'll dry quick. Only ones I got.

The sun is headed down; I'd better move on out of here. I set the pack on the bike carrier, drape the wet clothes over the pack to dry, and bungee cord it all tight to the bike.

Jane comes out of the motor home, also in dry clothes. I go over to her and say, "Thanks again for your help with the bike. Guess I'll hit the road."

Her mouth sinks in disappointment. "Where are you going?"

"Not sure. Somewhere north."

"So you're wandering?" she asks.

"Sort of."

"That's a great thing for a young person to do. See what's out there in the world. When I was your age, I traipsed across Europe and India, even hitchhiked. But those were different times."

"Aren't you doing that now—traveling around seeing the sights?" I ask.

"Actually not. This trip is for something quite specific."

I don't want to come right out and ask, but I look at her

questioningly.

"I'm looking for water," she continues.

"Seems everybody's doing that. Do you have a drill rig inside?"

She laughs. "No, I'm looking for it in another way. Have you ever heard of a vision quest?" She stands with her weight on one foot and the other stretched behind her. Her chin is raised, and she peers up at me, mouth closed, green eyes bright. She's about six inches shorter than me.

I shake my head.

"It's from the Native Americans. Some of them can see things in visions, then go out and find them in reality."

"And you had a vision?"

She nods. "A way to stop the drought. I saw where the water is. The water for the whole continent has retreated, sunk down into a huge underground sea. It's blocked up down there, can't flow out, because we've messed up the natural cycle. That's what's causing the drought. Ordinarily the rain falls to earth, seeps through the soil, collects underground, and then flows out into springs and rivers and lakes. There it evaporates, forms clouds, and falls back to earth. Simple and beautiful. But we've screwed up the climate so much that it doesn't flow anymore. It didn't just disappear, though. It's down there."

"And you're trying to find it."

"I'm trying to find the place where it's closest to the surface. Most of it has sunk too deep in the earth. But in the vision I saw a place where it rises up, gets close enough so we could tap it and get it flowing again."

"And that place is here?"

"No. I thought it might be, but it's not. When I got here, I could feel there's no huge source beneath it, just the ordinary shrinking water table."

"You felt that? How can you feel something like that?"

"I feel it in meditation, the same way I had the vision. When

I'm deep in meditation, I can tune in to the water, picture it in my mind—where it is, how much is there, how deep it is. Not exactly, but a general sense."

This reminds me of Cora. "I heard some people can do things like that. But I don't see how it can work."

"The way I do it is to bring my mind down to the transcendental level, where everything is connected. There I can connect to the water and know about it. That's how I got the vision of the huge underground sea where all the water has gone. And that's how I could tell that this isn't the place where it's close to the surface."

I don't know what to make of this. I've always sort of liked nutty ideas, but this is pushing it. "So what are you going to do now?"

"Go someplace else," she says determinedly.

"Where?" I ask.

"Death Valley."

I picture dry skulls in desert sand. "Why there?"

"That's the place deepest below sea level in all of North America. I thought it might be low enough to be close to the water."

"I don't think it's there," I blurted.

"Why not?"

"It doesn't seem like a place for water."

"Not even deep underground?"

"Could be. But I doubt it."

"Where do you think it is?" she asks.

"I wish I knew...but I don't."

"You want to go look for it?"

I don't know what to say. I'm surprised she asked. I guess she senses this because she continues, "Once I find the water, I may need some help."

"What are you going to do?"

"Find a way to get it flowing again, bring it to the surface so people can use it. Then the rivers and lakes will fill up again. The water will evaporate and fall back to earth—we'll have rain, even snow."

It sounds impossible to do that, but I don't want to tell her. Instead I say, "Sounds great. But you're headed east, and I wanted to go north."

Disappointment returns to her face. "You're right. It was just an idea." She manages a smile. "Well...enjoy your trip."

"Thanks. I hope you find your water."

"So do I."

I want to shake her hand, but that doesn't seem right with a lady. There should be some better way to say good-bye, but I don't know what. "Well, hope I see you again."

"So do I."

"'Bye."

"G'bye."

We both give a little wave. "Thanks again for helping me with the fire ants," I say.

"Glad to do it."

I strap on my helmet, start the bike, and drive away with a dip of my head and a flick of my hand. The sun is halfway down over the ragged Sierra horizon, and I want to make time while there's still some light.

After half a mile, though, the bike starts sputtering like it's out of gas. It coughs and dies, and I coast over to the shoulder. I shake it and hear the slosh of gas in the tank. Maybe getting banged on the ground broke something. All the wiring seems to be in place. Must be something inside. I swear at Gene for breaking it. Miles from any garage. Have to camp out here, figure out what to do in the morning. What a drag. Asphalt hot and sticky, smells of tar. Land by the road covered with junk— old tires, bottles, cans, plastic bags, paper—then just sand with a withered bush here and there. Desolate. I thought it was bad in Long Beach. I hate this world! Why does it have to be this way?

Have to push the bike off the road, find some place without fire ants.

Rumble of a car coming. No, it's the Winnebago, headlights on in the dusk. Stops behind me, flashers on. Jane gets out. "Trouble?"

"Yeah." A disgusted shrug. "Something's broken, don't know what."

"Well, there's a garage in the town of Death Valley. If you want, you can put the bike on the back, and we'll drop it off there in the morning."

Saved! "Thank you, that would be great. I was going to camp out over there someplace, push it for miles in the morning."

She shakes her head and smiles. "No need for that. Put it on the carrier in the back and get in."

"Thanks, I appreciate it."

A Winnebago is about as far from a motorcycle as you can get. Big comfy seats you sink down into, soft ride like floating along, huge windshield so the world looks like a big-screen TV, dashboard full of dials and lights, a computer monitor with satellite navigation and internet, cell phone, fold-out shelves for drinks and food. It's its own little world. And it's brand new—can tell by the smell. Jane is perched like a queen on a throne, handling the steering wheel while the cruise control handles the gas.

I like her, but I'm not sure what to make of her. She acts and dresses relaxed and casual, doesn't play the "I'm the older person, the authority figure" game. She's definitely not a high school teacher. Being around her, I don't feel like a kid but a regular person. It's almost like we're the same age, or no age. But there's also something dignified and old fashioned about her. She moves gracefully and talks like a fine lady.

She asks me about home and school, but I don't have much to say about it. Graduated last week into no future.

She tells me about her life, which is a lot more interesting than mine, maybe because there's been more of it. She grew up in Connecticut and went to law school there, then worked as a lawyer for poor people in LA. She learned how to be a meditation teacher in India. She was married for a while but didn't have kids. Now she's retired and raises roses in Pacific Palisades.

It's late by the time we get to the RV park in Death Valley. There's hardly anyone else here—not surprising for June. A few shadowy palm trees around the edge of the park looking like forearms and hands sticking out of the sand. The night is hot and clear and strewn with stars. I set up my tent on the ground next to her Winnebago, hoping it's not on a fire ant nest, or if it is, the floor of the tent will keep them out. It's a blue dome tent, and I've hiked with it in the San Bernadino Mountains, Catalina Island, and the Anza-Borrego Desert east of San Diego. It's a friend. So are the pack, air mattress, sleeping bag, stove, cook kit, and canteen. I spread the bag on the mattress—too hot to sleep in it— and lie down on top. I hope Jane is as cozy as I am. I hope my parents and sister are doing OK—all tucked into their rockabye beds in the little house on the edge of the salty ocean. And me floating on air deep in the valley of the shadow of death.

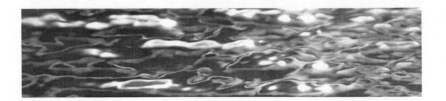

In the morning I wash up in the comfort station, and before it gets too hot I work on the bike. The fuel pump is broken. The garage here probably doesn't have that part, or if they do, they'll charge me a fortune for it. I'd be better off waiting until I get to a town big enough to have a discount auto parts store. Maybe I can ride with Jane until then.

Only one section of the RV park is open, because so few people come in the summer. On one side of us is a pickup truck with a silver trailer that has a Good Sam Club sticker and a "No Knockin' When It's Rockin'" sign on the door. On the other side is a van with "Just Married" painted on the back. From the bumper hangs a piece of cord where someone had probably tied tin cans. Spending your honeymoon in a van in Death Valley doesn't sound romantic, but that's all a lot of people can afford.

The ranger comes around to collect for the overnight stay—twenty-five dollars per vehicle. Since the motorcycle's a vehicle, it gets charged too, she says. She looks to be right out of college, blonde and blue eyed, a bit like my sister. I tell her I'm traveling in the RV and the bike is broken.

Jane comes out in a robe—she must've heard us talking. She confirms that we're together and the bike goes on the back of the RV. The ranger says OK, and Jane pays her.

I wish I could pay, but twenty-five dollars is a lot, especially since I have to buy the fuel pump. I wish I could go to college like the ranger and get a good job. But even a college degree doesn't mean you'll get a good job.

I thank Jane for paying for both of us.

"Not a problem," she says. "I'd have to pay the same even if it was just me. How's the motorcycle?"

I explain about the fuel pump and ask if I can ride with her until we get to an auto parts store.

"Sure," she says with a smile. "Let me get dressed, and we'll have some breakfast."

I thank her, then feel awkward about thanking her all the time.

She comes out in few minutes carrying a tray with tea, granola, yogurt, bowls, and spoons. I contribute raisins and almonds from my pack, and she thanks *me* this time. We eat in a picnic area shaded by a wooden roof bleached gray from the sun. The few palm trees seem to be drooping. In between them are spear-tufted yucca crowns and creosote bushes dripping resin in the swelter.

As we're finishing breakfast, a middle-aged couple get out of the trailer and a young couple out of the van, both looking sleepy but happy.

Jane gathers up our bowls and spoons. "Pack 'em up and move 'em out," she says in a funny cowboy accent. Wearing faded jeans, a blue work shirt, and a straw sun hat, she looks like a small cowboy. "We're goin' to Badwater!"

We drive away, already glad of the air conditioning. When she takes off her hat, I'm surprised to see her hair is all gray—first time I've seen it in the light. It's gathered up on top, held with a turquoise-studded silver clip. I'd thought she was about my mom's age, but even grandma's hair isn't all gray and she's sixty-one. Could Jane be older than that? Her skin doesn't look old, it's not wrinkled. Maybe she's not old but had some terrible fright that turned it all white. I read that can happen.

The wind is sweeping sand across the two-lane highway, blurring the center line, and stirring up dust devils out on the flats. Farther out, bare ridges loom like gray-backed sleeping dinosaurs above gullies cut out by vanished rivers. The wind is busy gnawing the land down to its skeleton, reducing buttes to rocky spars and pinnacles, strewing their dirt across the flats in wavy patterns like a dry ocean. The glare of the sun drains the landscape of color. Only the wind and sand move. Death Valley is like a superheated version of the moon. I don't see any dry skulls, but I don't see any living animals either. Just us.

"I was here once before, twenty-six years ago," Jane says. "A bunch of us came out at New Year's to celebrate the new millennium. We camped out and had a big party. Weather was great."

Frowning, she shakes her head. "California—the whole country—has changed a lot since then, gotten even dryer and hotter, fewer plants and animals. But this place hasn't changed. It was just as desolate back then. The difference is that the desolation has spread. What we see here is the future for the rest of the world—a bunch of lifeless minerals—unless we bring nature back into flow again, get that underground sea up to the surface so it can restart the cycle of circulation."

That seems like a big job for one person—or two, or anybody—to do.

We drop down into the Badwater Basin, a deep crevasse between two mountain ranges. The lowest point in North America turns out to be a parking lot. A few cars sit on the edge of an expanse of what looks like dirty snow but is actually slabs of salt cracked into strange honeycomb shapes. No water—bad or otherwise—to be seen. A sign announces that we're 282 feet below sea level. The air is heavy and hard to breathe, the opposite of a mountaintop. The sun, too intense to look at, seems to fill the sky, turning it into a griddle above our heads.

"This is grim," Jane says, putting on her sun hat. "No shade to meditate in. I'll have to do it out in the sun. I can almost feel my skin mutating into melanomas."

She lays the folded blanket on the ground and sits on it cross-legged. Then she picks something up. "Look—a sea shell!"

Sure enough. Half the home of an ancient clam, chalky and

gritty.

"This wasn't always desert," she says. "Maybe it will change again."

I imagine all this being under water, us too, chatting with the clam about the weather.

"I'll be here about twenty minutes," Jane says. "You can take a walk or take a nap or anything you want. But quiet. I need to go deep." She straightens her back and closes her eyes. It doesn't look very comfortable.

I don't know what to do. It's too hot to walk, I'm not tired enough to sleep. I go back to the Winnebago and sit inside where it's not so hot. Close my eyes. Maybe I can go deep too.

But I don't. I end up just sitting there wishing I was listening to grandpa's old records.

After a while Jane comes back shaking her head. "Nothing. Well, I struck out twice now. Where do you think we can get close to all the water?"

"Yosemite!" I say.

"OK, we'll try it. At least it'll be cooler than this...and prettier."

We head north at 10 a.m. on roads shimmering with heat mirages that make the concrete look wet. The AC is going full blast, but we can still feel the heat streaming down from the roof. Jane points to a thermos bottle in the one of the wells of the drink stand. "Would you like some hot water?"

"Sure," I say, thinking she's joking and really means ice water.

"Good. Pour us a couple of cups."

I do, and it actually *is* hot water. I hand her a steaming cup. "You're really going to drink that?"

She takes the cup with a nod. "Hot water is the best thing to drink...especially in hot weather. It warms you up inside so you're in better balance with the outside, not so big a contrast."

"How about coffee?" I ask.

"Never touch the stuff."

"What do you do when you're tired?"

"Sleep."

I have to admit it makes sense, but I yawn, having missed my morning coffee. To the left dry hills, to the right dry flatlands. For hours. Jane starts to yawn too.

As we're rolling through Lone Pine, we pass an auto parts store, but it's closed. Most of the stores are closed: Sunday. Forgot about that. "Can I stick with you a bit longer?" I ask.

"Sure."

I'm actually glad, and I think she is too.

"If you want to take a break, I'll be glad to drive," I volunteer.

She looks at me skeptically. "You ever driven anything this big?"

"I've driven vans. I used to work for a scuba diving school, and I'd drive the van with the gear out to the dive spot. That was actually more complicated than this because it had a gear shift."

"This is so much bigger than a van. You have to be particularly careful when you're turning, to swing out far enough to make the turn but still not hit someone in the other lane. And you need a lot more room to pass, especially if someone's coming in the other direction. When you pull back in, you have to make sure the car you passed is behind you. And don't even try to parallel park. Find a place where you can pull straight in."

She's going to let me do it! Great!

"You're yawning, too, though," she says. Maybe we'd better get you some coffee. Normally I'm against drugs, but we need to keep you awake. It's about time for lunch anyway."

We stop at a Denny's, and she gives me more instructions on parking. As soon as we get out, the oven blast hits me, and I start to sweat. But inside it's too cool, and I shiver.

She orders the vegetarian special, a noodle-cheese-tomato-zucchini glop, and I order a double cheeseburger and fries. When the check comes, I'm finishing a piece of pumpkin pie with whipped cream and a second cup of black coffee. I reach for my wallet, but she picks up the check and says, "If you're driving for me, I'll pay for the food."

"Wow, thanks! That's really nice of you." And I mean it. I need to stretch my cash out.

Back at the Winnebago, she hands me the keys. "We'll give it a try. Just be careful."

"I will."

I adjust the seat and mirrors, and she explains the controls and gadgets. I back it out with her sitting nervously in the passenger seat. It's more like driving a bus than a car. I'd like to switch on the radio or play a CD, but she didn't have music on, so I don't ask.

After a half hour of watching me she says, "You seem to be able to handle it. Just don't go too fast. If you get a ticket, you have to pay it yourself."

"OK, I'll be careful." I lean back and roll along, feeling like the king of the road...or the captain of a ship...hopefully not the *Titanic*.

We pass a highway patrol car parked on the shoulder with lights flashing, then a truck he had stopped. It's Gene and Cora's truck, the same tanker with a trailer on the back.

"Uh oh," Jane says. "So he gets in trouble after all."

"I wonder if he was just speeding...or did the cops find out they were pumping water?"

"Well, let's not go back and ask him," she says.

"Yeah, I can't feel too sorry for him."

She wants to trade off the driving every hour, so neither of us gets too tired. I'd rather keep on wheeling it, but they're her wheels.

I'm driving again as we get to Lee Vining, where we stop for a break. I pull in and park by the rest rooms. In the rearview mirror I see Gene's truck pulling up behind us, blocking us off. He swings down from the cab and walks towards us, arms bent at the elbows. My heart starts pounding, and I lock the doors.

Gene tries the door, then pounds his fist on the window, round face red, mustache twitching. "You bastard, you ratted us out to the cops!"

"I never! We didn't call them," I say.

"Sure, you say that now that I got you." Gene's furious sputtering leaves spit on the window.

"Look," I tell him, "what you did to my bike was rotten. But I wouldn't turn you in for drilling water."

"Then why did we get stopped? We weren't speeding. Now our license plate goes onto the list. They'll stop us whenever they see us."

Jane leans over and tells him in a calm but forceful voice, "Maybe your rig looked suspicious to them. Could be they're stopping everyone with a tanker truck now, especially if you've got a trailer on the back. We didn't call them." She holds up her cell phone. "But we're going to call them *now*, if you don't leave us alone."

Gene starts to say something, then glares at us and stalks back to his truck.

After they leave we go to the rest rooms, but I'm too nervous to pee.

Back in the Winnebago Jane says, "What a thoroughly unpleasant man. But some of it is because things are so terrible now. People are under so much pressure...they do things they maybe otherwise wouldn't do. In another situation he might be OK."

This makes sense, but I'm not really in the mood to hear anything good about Gene. I start the engine, but somehow I put the gear selector in drive rather than reverse. When I hit the gas, the RV lurches forward, bounces over the concrete block in front of the parking space, and hits the side of the building with a crunch. Something behind us inside falls with a crash.

Jane cries out and covers her face with her hands. I want to disappear...or die. I can't believe I did something so dumb. "I'll back it off."

"No, you won't," Jane says icily. "You've done quite enough already. Turn off the engine."

We check behind us and see her pots of aloe vera and African violets have fallen from the windowsill into the kitchen sink but aren't broken. We get out and see the lower front edge of the Winnebago is crumpled and discolored from the red brick wall. The wall itself is OK, except for a smear of beige paint.

"I'll pay for it," I say, then realize I can't begin to pay for it. My breath is coming in quick shallow pants.

Jane's face is lined. She suddenly looks old. I can feel how mad she is at me. I can't blame her—crashing her brand-new motor home. How could I have put it in the wrong gear? I'd like to just float away from here, from everything...most of all from myself.

Jane closes her eyes, breathes out with a sigh, breathes in slowly, then looks at me, her mouth wrinkled as the Winnebago. "OK, it's done. My home on wheels isn't new anymore. It's battered like all of us."

"I can see why you'd be mad about it," I say.

"Yes, I am mad. I bought it just for this trip. The first dent in anything new is hard to take. But I could've done it myself."

"I'd like to be able to pay for it, but I don't have enough money." My hands are trembling.

Jane bends down and pulls on the crumpled edge, but it doesn't move. "At least it's not going to fall off. We'll leave it. I don't want to pay for it, and the insurance won't cover it because it's less than the deductible. So be it."

"Thanks for being so nice about it."

"Well, you were under a lot of pressure. You got confused and had an accident. It happens." She gives me a wry look. "But I'm not going to let you drive again until you calm down."

I nod while squeezing my hands together to stop the trembling.

"That guy really threw you off, didn't he? You're still a nervous wreck."

"Guess so." I can barely speak, my throat is so pinched.

"You're really angry at him, aren't you?" she says.

"Yeah."

"That's understandable, considering how he acted. What would you like to do to him?"

I'm relieved to be talking about something besides the crash, but I don't know what to make of these questions. I'm too upset to think, so I just shrug and answer, "Punch him in the face. But he's bigger than me."

"So he was threatening you and you were afraid of him."

I don't want to admit I was afraid of him, but I'd rather do that than talk about the RV, so I say, "Yeah, something like that."

Her voice is gentle now. "Can you see he was also afraid...of the police, of losing his business...and what might happen to his family then? That might also be why he lied to me and then broke your motorcycle. He was afraid, so he took it out on other people—that's happening a lot now. People pass their stress around like a hot potato. He tosses his on you, you get mad and make a mistake with the gears. Then I get mad at you."

"You don't seem mad now, though."

"No, not anymore. It helps to see the reasons why people do things. Then you can step back from it a bit, not be overwhelmed by it, let it go." She glances at her watch. "But now we need to go, get on the road again."

We both look at the front edge then at each other. I shrug apologetically, she shrugs forgivingly, and we get back in the Winnebago.

I'd like to keep the convo away from the crash, so as she's pulling out of the parking lot, I ask, "How did things get so terrible? Why are people always fighting one another?"

I can tell Jane likes to talk about stuff like this. Her face brightens and she grits her teeth a bit. "That's the kind of society we live in, where the things people need—food, shelter, clothing, water, fuel, medicine—are owned by someone else, and we have to buy those things from them with money." She glances at me while she's driving. "That means the people who own those things end up with a huge amount of money, and the rest of us have to fight each other to get enough. That system produces people who think that's natural, who fit into it and can win at it— good fighters. But they're cut off from other people, afraid somebody else is going to take things from them. The only thing real to them is money. So they end up abusing the planet, ruining the climate, destroying the natural balance."

"Where did you learn this?" I ask. "Did you study this kind of stuff in school?"

Jane shakes her head and gives a short laugh. "No, they don't teach this in school. I learned it from the inside, from seeing how it works, how people get rich. My grandfather got rich in the First World War. He owned a small company that made fertilizer, and he converted that into making explosives. He got a government contract, and it became a big company. My father took it over and got even richer in the Second World War. But he could see their kind of explosives were getting obsolete. New kinds were being developed that he couldn't compete with. So he sold the company. He got all his money together and thought, *What do people need*? Well, a place to live. So he bought real estate, apartment buildings in Hartford, Connecticut. We lived in a great big house. Even had an indoor swimming pool. Had a tennis court, but that was outside. A barn in back with horses and a big field to ride. A cook, a maid, a gardener.

"The buildings he owned were full of factory workers—two or three rooms for a family. Back then there weren't public swimming pools and tennis courts where they could go. But we had our own. There were hardly any parks. But we had our own.

"My father and his rich friends had lots of influence with the city council, and they used that to stop the city from building pools and parks because that would raise their taxes.

"Our tenants worked long and hard for low wages to pay us rent. And to pay the grocery store owner. And the clothing store owner. And finally the undertaker."

"Sounds like my family."

"What do you parents do?"

"My dad's a car mechanic and mom's a waitress."

"Do they rent or own?"

"Rent."

"That's it—they're locked onto a treadmill that generates money for other people but not for them."

"Yeah, seems that way. How did you get to see all this?"

"From what it did to my father." The spirit fades from her face. Her cheeks sink and a web of wrinkles shows on them. "Money was his whole life, and he was very good at getting it. But the business got boring to him. He wanted to get money in a more exciting way than just raising rents. He started to gamble— high stakes. He lost but couldn't quit. Lost millions of dollars, had to sell apartment buildings to pay his debts, but he still couldn't quit." She pauses, takes a deep breath, and releases it as a sigh. Her eyes glisten. "Finally he killed himself. Left a note saying this was the only way to keep the family from going bankrupt."

"How old were you then?"

"Seventeen. About the same as you."

"I'm eighteen. It must've been hard for you."

"It was. I was the one who found him. It was a Sunday morning, and we were supposed to go to church. I was looking all over the house for him and finally found him in the garage— hanging in the garage." She bites her lip.

"Whew. Awful," I say.

"I was angry at him for doing that, but later when I learned how this system operates, how it mangles everyone in it, I could understand him better. I started to see that we have to change it...before the whole world commits suicide."

"How, though?"

The energy returns to her face. Her upper lip lifts enough to show the edges of small, even teeth. "We have to take the world—the natural resources, the factories, the banks—away from the rich and make them the common property of us all. Then we can use those things to meet human needs instead of just making profits for the owners."

"They put people like you in jail," I say with a laugh.

"I've been in jail! But you can usually buy your way out of jail, if you've got money. And my father died well before he gambled away all the money."

"What were you in jail for?"

"Criminal trespass and conspiracy. I was representing some workers who were trying to form a union. The company fired them all and hired scabs, but the workers occupied the plant and refused to leave. I brought them food and blankets and stuff, and we discussed legal strategy. The cops raided the plant and arrested us all." Her face pinches at the memory.

"I testified that I was just there to give them legal advice. What I didn't know was that the company had an agent among the strikers, and he said I'd also brought supplies, given them material assistance. Since occupying the building was illegal, giving them material assistance was also illegal, so I was charged with conspiracy. The guy's testimony contradicted mine, showed I was lying, so the DA charged me also with perjury, which meant I could be disbarred from practicing law. It looked pretty grim. But the company didn't want to reveal the identity of the agent, because then he wouldn't be of any more use to them. That meant he couldn't appear in court, so the DA had to drop the perjury charge. The judge gave me and all the strikers ninety days for trespassing and defying a court order. In jail I started helping prisoners file legal complaints against conditions there, so they put me in solitary. That's supposed to be hard punishment, but I just meditated the whole time.

"I was also arrested for trespassing and failure to disperse during three demonstrations. One of them was right near Long Beach—the Naval Weapons Station."

"I know that place—a big gate with guards. When were you there?"

"That was during the war on Iraq, before you were born. They had depleted uranium stored there, a terribly cruel weapon, and a bunch of us stormed the gate to protest it. The navy cops grabbed us, pepper sprayed us all, and beat up some of the men.

"Another time at a sit-in at the immigration service against deportations. And for occupying a park in Santa Monica that the state wanted to tear up for a freeway onramp. They corralled us in with plastic mesh and then for laughs threw a tear gas grenade next to us."

I can't believe this sweet old lady is telling me about all her arrests. "You've had quite a life.

"It hasn't always been pleasant," she says, "but I don't have any regrets. I've always wanted to change things, and some people don't like that."

"I like it."

"Good."

Jane drives over the Tioga Pass, the east entrance to Yosemite. The Winnebago is weak on hills; we're lugging at thirty m.p.h. The sun is setting over the Sierras, shooting rays of golden light through the haze, shining the clouds pink and violet. With a last gleam it drops behind the mountains and lights them from behind into miles of blue craggy peaks.

It's dark by the time we get to the campground. I like it much better here than the desert—the air is cool and fresh, and I can pitch my tent under a tree.

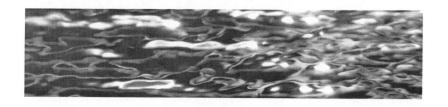

I wake up several times in the night to the sound of little things falling onto the taut nylon of the tent. *Raindrops!* I go back to sleep with a smile.

In the morning everything is still dry. Instead of rain, the tent and ground are strewn with pine needles. The tree above me is shedding needles and small branches as it withers. Its bark is gray and flaky, limbs limp.

Jane hasn't come out of the motor home yet, so I take a walk to the nearby Tuolumne River, which turns out to be a meandering creek about six inches deep. The meadows on both sides are brown.

I stroll in the Sequoia grove among trees soaring over two hundred feet towards the sky with massive trunks as wide as a house. Some are over a thousand years old. But they won't get any older—an army of dead soldiers left standing at attention.

By the time I get back, Jane is setting out breakfast on a picnic table. Before, her gray hair was always pinned up, but now it flows halfway down her back. She has lots of it, and it looks good against her lavender blouse. She seems a little down, and I'm worried she may still be mad at me. Then she says, "Bad news, but not a surprise. No deep source of water here either. I didn't get any hint of it in my meditation."

"So much for my guess," I say, disappointed. "What's yours?"

"Not sure. I've run out of intuition. We'll just keep going north and see what we find."

She's saying "we," so I guess I'm forgiven.

Breakfast cheers both of us up, and we (Jane at the wheel— she hasn't totally forgiven me) drive into Yosemite Valley, the main part of the park. I remember the pictures I've seen of it, taken before the drought: Bridal Veil and Yosemite Falls with tons of white water cascading over granite cliffs, crashing down into deep pools on the canyon floor that's covered with verdant grass and ferns.

But now the glaciers have melted and snow and rain are rare, so the falls are thin ribbons of water spilling over the cliffs then trickling through brown grass into what used to be the Merced River. We hear an occasional bird, but we don't see them or any other animals. Jane finds a blue jay feather, which she sticks in her hair—but the jay is probably dead. We're very quiet as we drive away from the park—as if we've been to Mother Nature's funeral.

Soon we're out of the mountains into the Central Valley—flat, hot, dry. I learned in school this is some of the best agricultural land in the world, growing everything from almonds to zucchinis. But that's changed now. Farmers have had to switch to low-water crops like millet and cotton. Many of the fields have been abandoned to weeds and cactus, and even the weeds are withering. There's a crash program to develop synthetic food, but the stuff tastes terrible. There's also a crash program to distill ocean water with nuclear heat, but the reactors leak. There's lots of crash programs now, but they're too late—the crash has already happened.

I can remember when it wasn't so bad. I can remember snow on Mt. Baldy in the winter, misty mornings in the spring, and how good rain felt after a hot day and how good the earth smelled afterwards, and how the robins pulled the worms out of the ground. I haven't seen a robin or a worm in years—just gulls and pelicans in Long Beach now. If it's gotten so bad so quick, what do I have to look forward to, what's the future going to be? Dry bones.

As I'm mulling this, a siren bursts the air behind us and lights careen off our mirrors. Jane gasps and grips the wheel tighter. I look behind and see a highway patrol car. *Glad I'm not driving*, I think as Jane pulls off to the side of the freeway, a frightened look on her face.

The cop stops behind us and turns off his siren but leaves the lights whirling. "Stand out of the vehicle!" he orders through a loudspeaker. We get out, and he strides towards us. Too many doughnuts have given him a doughnut around the waist, highlighted by a belt crammed with the tools of his trade—pistol, club-flashlight, handcuffs, and pepper spray. "See your driver's license. Both of you."

We give him our licenses, and he types the numbers into a gadget from his belt.

"Why did you stop us?" Jane asks.

He looks at her a moment, tongue pressing behind his lip, then says, "We have reason to believe you may be engaged in illegal drilling and theft of water. I'll need to examine the vehicle."

Gene again!

"This is an RV," Jane says. "Where could we hide the water?"

"RVs are often used to conceal drilling rigs."

"Do you have a search warrant?"

"I don't need a warrant to examine the vehicle. All I need is probable cause," he replies impatiently. "I see you have an arrest record."

"Yes, and proud of it."

I've never heard anyone talk to the police this way. She comes up to his chest and weighs half as much as he does, but she stands her ground, green eyes peering defiantly up at him. I like her spirit, but it makes me nervous. I don't want to get an arrest record. Hard enough to get a job without one.

The cop scowls. "I can either inspect the vehicle now and send you on your way, or I take you both into custody, have the vehicle towed into Stockton, and inspect it there."

"Do it now," she says, stepping away from the door.

He climbs inside, and Jane and I exchange nervous glances while a lizard scurries over the gravel beside the road and cars and trucks blast past. The cop comes back out and says, "You're free to go." Jane nods but says nothing, and he strides back to his car.

As Jane drives away, she says, "So your former boss takes revenge."

"What a rotten guy," I say. "Maybe it makes him feel better."

In smoggy, dusty Modesto we pass a line of people a block long waiting in front of a food bank. Since the drought, the price of food has soared and people have less money to buy it with. All the fuel burned to ship it here is worsening the climate change. Spiral of doom.

We also pass an auto parts store, and Jane looks at me inquiringly. "You want to stop?"

At first I don't know what to say, and she slows down. I hadn't thought about it—guess I pushed it out of my mind. Now I have to decide. "No," I blurt. "I'd like to keep on with you. What if I gave you the money the fuel pump would cost—probably about ninety dollars. That won't repair the dent, but it'll buy some gas."

"OK," Jane says with a smile. "If you want to do it that way, we can."

"I'd like to find that water."

"We'll do it."

I'm surprised by what I just said, but somehow it seems right. I'm glad, too, that she accepted the money. It's not like I'm a kid.

"You're still very tense, though," she says. "Before you can drive again, you're going to need to relax. The best way to do that would be to meditate."

The idea of driving again sounds great, but I'm not sure about meditating. "Could I meditate?"

"Sure you could."

"Isn't it hard?"

"No, it's easy."

"How would I do it?"

"If you want to, I'll teach you."

"OK."

She pulls off the freeway at a rest stop. "What you're going to learn is Transcendental Meditation. Let's go into the back."

Out of a drawer near the dining nook, she takes some small brass bowls and candlesticks and a picture of an old guy in an orange blanket. She fills the bowls with rice and water, lights a candle and incense, and starts singing a song in a strange language to the picture. It's weird but interesting. The song makes me quiet inside. I just stand beside her watching. She stops singing and whispers a sound to me, then motions me to repeat it. I do, and she tells me to sit in a chair, close my eyes, and think it silently. The sound expands into the space behind my closed eyes, then contracts into a pulsing spark of light in the darkness. My breath and heartbeat slow. I seem to be beyond my skin, filling the whole RV. The sound is floating through me, sometimes faster, sometimes slower, then long and stretched out. I feel like I'm sinking into the chair, then into the earth. I want to hold on, to keep from disappearing, but something tells me to let everything go. I free-fall through space, then realize it's impossible to fall because there's no down. I'm hovering...like a dragonfly. The sound gets fainter and finer and finally disappears. I have no thoughts, but I know I'm here. I seem to extend beyond the RV, then beyond all space and boundaries to unite with everything. For a moment I know I am everything, the whole universe, but as soon as I think, *I'm everything*, I'm not anymore. I'm just Bob Parks sitting in a chair in an RV outside of Lodi.

"Slowly open the eyes," Jane says.

When I do, she's smiling at me. I smile back.

"It's easy?" she asks.

"Yes."

"Good, let's close our eyes and continue."

I do, but it doesn't come back. I'm just sitting here thinking a sound, hearing the rumble of the freeway, wondering when we eat lunch, needing to itch my ear. Then I think about how Mr. Kramer, my English teacher, would correct that and say, "You need to *scratch* your ear because it itches." I think about the books we read in his class and how much I liked them.

"Slowly let's open our eyes," Jane says.

I look at her; she's still smiling. Green eyes and gray hair—you'd think that'd be cold, but it's not. It sparkles. Maybe that's because she meets your eyes.

"How was it?" she asks.

"Not as good."

"Sometimes it's that way. We can go very deep one time and next time stay more on the surface. It depends on how our nervous system is. How do you feel now?"

"Well...quieter, more relaxed but energetic. I like it."

"Excellent. This will also help us find the water."

"How's that?" I ask.

"Because water and consciousness are a lot alike. But the explanation is a bit complicated." She tips her head to the side, thinks a moment, and says, "We go deep into our consciousness in meditation. There we're connected to everything in the universe, because that's what the universe is, consciousness expressing itself in different forms. Consciousness is the invisible essence that makes up the universe.

"And water is somewhat like that. Water is the basic component of life. Animals and plants are composed mainly of water, but we don't see that. Our body is mostly water, but we see only the solid outer form. A tree is mostly water. It draws it from the earth and turns it into the colorless sap, which then becomes green leaves and branches.

"Similarly, we can't see the field of consciousness, but it's the basic component of the universe. It manifests into energy and matter. Have you heard of the unified field?"

"It's something in physics, right?"

"Right. Physics has found that matter isn't really the basis of the universe. Matter is continually emerging out of and dissolving back into energy. And that energy comes out of the unified field, which is invisible and non-material, consciousness manifesting itself as the physical universe.

"When we meditate, we bring our awareness to the deepest level of our mind, where it connects with the unified field. It's like diving down through the ocean of our mind until we reach the bottom, the source. And our awareness draws energy from that deep source. We bring that energy back to the surface with us, back into activity, so we think better and act better. The more contact we have with the unified field, the more energetic and healthful and successful we are. But when we lose contact with it, we make mistakes and suffer.

"It's similar with the tree. If it can't contact the water and draw it up, it withers. The water is there, but the tree can't reach it. The contact is broken, so it doesn't flow.

"That's what we have now in the world. People are out of contact with their inner source, so their life is a mess. They've injured the climate of the earth, damaged the natural cycles, so water is locked deep inside the earth and doesn't reach the surface. The land is drying up and life is withering."

This sort of makes sense to me, but a different kind of sense than what I'm used to. "But I still don't understand how meditation will help us find the water."

Jane leans towards me and gestures with her hands. "The unified field is where everything in the universe becomes one. When we bring our minds to it, we're connected with everything, including the water. We can sense it. And when two people, better yet a whole group, bring their minds to the unified field, they're all joined, and that strengthens the effect for everyone. If we meditate together, we have a better chance of sensing where the water is."

I'm not sure what to say. "Uh well, to tell you the truth...it sounds...a little nutty. But maybe that's why I like it. It's nutty enough that it just might work. We've tried all the regular ways. Let's try this one."

"I'm glad you want to try it. When you experience it more, you'll see it's not so nutty," Jane says. "I can tell you're already calmer. You want to try driving again?"

I'm amazed, not expecting this. "Sure! I'll be very careful."

"I'm sure you will. And I'll be watching very carefully."

I roll it out of the rest area and back onto the freeway, feeling totally different—light and happy.

But outside in the Central Valley things aren't light and happy. People in their cars have a tight, pressured look on their faces, and they drive angrily, honking if they think you're going too slow and giving you the finger as they pass.

I read that with all the crop failures most farmers are almost broke. To stay in business, a lot of them sold the mineral and deep water rights under their land to the corporations. They're allowed to have a private well down to 100 feet, and at first that gave enough water for crop irrigation. But now the water table in the valley has dropped so far that there's almost no water at that level. And drilling deeper take special equipment they can't afford...plus they'd get fined if they got caught.

The corporations have adapted oil-drilling technology to sink wells 1000 feet down and pump the last water out of the aquifers. They can drill right on the farmer's land, then sell him the water—if he can afford to buy it.

As I'm thinking about all this, I get mad. "Tell me something," I say to Jane. "How could people let things get so bad? I mean, didn't they know something like this would happen if they kept doing like they were doing? There must've been some warning signs. Why didn't they change?"

Jane thinks for a moment, tenting her fingers together. "Because people don't run the system. The system runs the people. And it demands ruthless competition. If the CEO of one company decides to put a higher priority on protecting the environment than on making profits, he's going to go out of business or lose his job. If one country requires their corporations to put the environment over profits, the corporations in the other countries are going to wipe them out. The changes would have to made globally, and the rich nations don't want to give the UN that kind of power.

"Another reason is that we've spent so much money on all these wars that we're almost broke. We can't afford to really take care of the environment, to correct global warming.

"So it's not just the water that's gone, blocked up inside the earth. The money's gone too, blocked up in a few hands. The people that have it are now closing in on the remaining water. They've bought up the rights in Canada, Scandinavia, Siberia.

"But the problem is even deeper than that. The basic problem—the one that's behind the water and the money—is that human consciousness is all blocked up, totally overstressed. The world has been at war now for over a hundred years. Since 1914 it's been constant military and economic warfare. For most of that time we've lived under the threat of nuclear annihilation— the whole show could end any day.

"Now we've made the planet sick. It's broken down, can't take the strain anymore. And we know if it goes down, we go down with it.

"We carry all this fear and anger around with us. The anxiety affects our brains—we can't think clearly enough to bring about the kind of changes that would solve the problem. The stress also affects our bodies—we get sick a lot, can't mobilize our energy."

My mouth sags and I shake my head. "Sounds hopeless, worse than I thought. I thought the problem was just the water."

"It's not hopeless," Jane says. "It's just that the solution has to come from the deepest level. It has to start in our consciousness."

"But how can we do that?"

"That's what Transcendental Meditation is for. It takes our ordinary thinking mind deep into our consciousness, down to the level where we're joined with the universal mind, the unified field. When we contact that energy, it heals our stresses so we can think and act better."

I try to get this, but it's pretty airy. I did feel something like that unified field in the meditation, though—everything being together. I'd like to go back there—especially when I look out at the world around us now.

Where we are is grim. Although the map shows mountain ranges on both sides of the valley, there's too much dust in the air to see them. We pass several tall drilling rigs like oil derricks, each surrounded by a high chain-link fence topped with barbed wire. On the fences are signs:

Chevron Aquatech
Leaders in Deep-Drilling Water Technology

No Trespassing!
Violators Prosecuted!

Some of the signs have been sprayed over; on others the word "kill" has been sprayed above "Chevron."

We pass lots of political billboards:

The Restore America Party
Bring Back Liberty and Prosperity

The Americans First Party
Fights for Citizen Rights

The One Nation Under God Party
Defend Our Sacred Heritage

We pass another tanker truck being inspected by the highway patrol.

"This is not the place to find the water," Jane says with a shake of her head. "Any water here has already been found. Things are too desperate. The Central Valley is turning into the Owens Valley, which is turning into Death Valley. Let's get out of here."

The drive is long...long...long...but finally we reach Redding, where the land starts to rise and scraggly trees take over the parched fields. By then it's almost dark, but Jane wants to press on. We climb into the foothills of the Cascade Range, and the air becomes cool and fresh enough so that we turn off the AC, open the windows, and enjoy the evening.

By the time we get to Dunsmuir we're exhausted from the long trek, so we stop for the night at an RV park. The ground is covered with concrete, though, with no place to stake down my tent. Then I realize I don't need a tent—no chance of rain...or mosquitoes. But I'm glad for the air mattress on the hard slab. I fall asleep wondering if the stars look brighter in the mountains because we're closer to them or because the air is clearer.

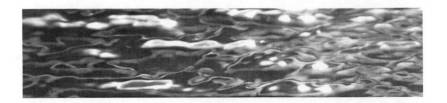

The sun wakes me early as it gleams on a dark pyramid soaring up from the horizon. I think I'm still dreaming, but then I realize it must be Mt. Shasta. It rises above us, smooth slopes slanting in an almost perfect cone up to the peak.

The RV park, though, is not so grand. It's crowded, and someone already has a radio on.

Jane comes out of her motor home, and her face lights up at the sight of the mountain. "Shasta! Beautiful. The holy mountain. It used to be covered with snow even in summer, but not anymore. It still has a glacier, the last one in California. And it's a real volcano, has a hot core deep down."

"I'd like to climb to the top."

"I bet you could do it. I'll stay here though," she says.

The sound of a television joins that of the radio, making a jangling mix.

"We should meditate," Jane says, "but not in this noise. Let's go somewhere else."

We head out with me driving and Jane giving directions from the navi. "We're right near the national forest. Let's try there. Should be quiet." The two-lane asphalt road is a welcome change from the six-lane concrete freeway. The hills are forested but the trees unhealthy—more gray than green with sagging branches. We find a shady glade with no campers and pull off the road there. Shasta is closer now, dominating the landscape, the lord of all it surveys. White veils of clouds are blowing around its peak.

Jane opens a storage cabinet and takes out blankets. "To sense the water we should be on the ground. You want to sit on a blanket?"

"How about my sleeping bag?" I ask.

"Fine."

We find a flat, grassy space shielded by trees from the sun and breeze. The ground is hard, even with the folded sleeping bag. I squirm around trying to get comfortable, but it doesn't seem to bother Jane, even though her blanket is thinner than my sleeping bag. She's sitting cross-legged with her feet tucked up onto her thighs. I try that but I'm too stiff. "How do you get the feet there like that?" I ask.

She sits up straighter with her hair streaming back, wearing loose cotton pants and a long-sleeved multi-colored shirt with no collar. "It took me ten years of yoga to loosen up enough to sit in full lotus. Don't worry about it. Just cross your legs."

"Should I think about finding water while I'm meditating?"

"No, just think your mantra very easily and be open to whatever happens. We'll meditate about twenty minutes. I'll watch the time."

I start the mantra, and it stretches out into a long hum, then breaks into pieces, each piece going with a heartbeat. It slows and goes with my breath. I think, how can I find the water if I don't think about it. Then I think about what we'll do with the water if we find it. Maybe we could get rich. What would I do with all the money? Then I realize I'm just sitting here having all these thoughts.

"Slowly let's open our eyes," Jane says.

"Was that twenty minutes?"

"Twenty-two."

"Felt like five."

"Any water?"

I shake my head.

"Me neither. But this is the Central Valley side of the mountain. Let's try the north side."

I drive back to the freeway and then north to Weed, where we stop for gas and groceries. Jane says she'll pay since I'm driving well again, and she tells me to pick what I want. I get a frozen pizza, some cans of ravioli and enchiladas, chocolate brownies, and a quart of Coke. At the checkout counter she opens her purse, looks through it, pauses with a worried frown, then looks again. "I had a fifty dollar bill in here. Now it's gone." She stares at me, then searches the purse again. "No, not here."

People in the line behind us are shuffling impatiently. She looks at me sharply, then says, "I'll use my credit card." She pulls the plastic out and pays, turning away from me. She walks stiffly back to the motor home, and I follow, carrying the groceries. *Does she think I stole it?*

Her face is strained as she turns to me. "I don't want to accuse you, Bob, but did you happen to take the money out of my purse? Maybe you needed something?"

I feel like I'm falling apart inside. How could she think that? "No! I didn't take it. I haven't touched your purse. I would never do anything like that."

"Well, where did it go?"

"I don't know—I never saw it." But how can I prove I didn't take it? How can I prove I'm not lying?

"Well, it's not there and it was there before."

"That doesn't mean I took it!"

"No, it doesn't. You're right. Maybe there's another explanation. But I don't see one." She turns her face away as tears run down her cheek.

I want to comfort her, but she wouldn't want to be comforted by a thief. I want to disappear, leap up to the top of Mt. Shasta. But I'm stuck here. "When was the last time you saw it?" I ask.

"Yesterday."

"And you didn't buy anything with it since then?"

"No."

"Maybe it'll turn up." Then I think maybe she'll interpret that as meaning since she caught me, I'll sneak the bill back, put it someplace where she'll find it. I can't stand this—there's no way out. If she really believes I took it, she'll suspect everything I say. "What do you want to do?" I ask her.

"Let's unload the groceries...and continue on." Her tears have stopped and she just looks depressed.

"Do you want to drive?" I ask her.

"You don't know how to use the navi. I need to give you directions."

I feel terrible but don't know what more to do or say. Both of us tense, we leave and she directs me over the back roads around the north side of the mountain. It looks different from here, the sides steeper, peak sharper.

"Let's try this place," she says as we pass a grove of trees. I pull off the road, and we bring out the blanket and sleeping bag to meditate on, both of us listless and avoiding the other's eyes.

It's pretty here—white-barked alder amid pine and fir, grass that's sparse but still has some green, wooded hills stretching north as far as we can see—but neither of us are in the mood to enjoy it. We sit far apart.

I can't really meditate—my mind is spinning in circles, and my back hurts from sitting without any support. Part of me would like to leave, but the bike is still broken. The thought of leaving is painful too. I didn't really know how much I've come to like being with Jane until this came along to ruin it. She'll probably always distrust me now, and there's nothing I can do about it. It makes me mad that she would think that of me. I'd be glad to give her fifty dollars if that would wipe the whole thing out. But it wouldn't. Then I think maybe the reason she's so upset isn't so much because of the money but because she likes being with me too and is sad that seems to be spoiled now. The whole mess is so hopeless that tears squeeze out of the sides of my eyes even though I try to hold them back.

"I found it!" Jane cries.

My body jerks from the sudden noise. *Oh, the water. I don't care about the water anymore. To hell with everything.*

Jane stands up as quickly as she can—not very—and walks as quickly as she can—also not very—into the Winnebago. *Maybe she's going to drive away and leave me, now that she's found the water.* She comes out a minute later crying and holding a fifty dollar bill. "I'm so sorry," she splutters as she rushes towards me. "I remembered in meditation. I hate to say this—to admit it—but I got paranoid and worried you might steal some money. So I hid it under the mattress. But deep down I was so ashamed of myself for thinking that that I blanked it out of my mind. All I knew was the money was gone. But *I* had taken it! Can you forgive me? Please, Bob. I'm so sorry. My memory isn't very good anymore. I'm seventy-seven years old and forget things sometimes." She shoved the bill at me. "Here, you should have the money."

I push it away. "I don't want the money. I just don't want you to think that I would steal it. You're paying for everything anyway. I don't need it." *Seventy-seven! I've never met anybody that old.*

She sits down beside me and speaks through quivering lips. "It was so terrible of me to do that."

I take her hand. "Well, you hardly know me. I'm just glad you found it." We each reach out to comfort the other and end up hugging and rocking back and forth.

"I hope we can put this behind us...maybe learn something from it," she snuffles.

I'm amazed by how relieved I am. I feel better than I would've if it hadn't happened.

She seems relieved too. "You forgive this foolish old woman?"

"Sure. You forgave me for smashing the RV. A lot of people wouldn't."

"But that was an accident. This was mean spirited on my part."

"I'm just glad everything is OK again," I say.

"Let's finish meditating."

"Good." This time I slide easily into the meditation. The

mantra is a whisper, my thoughts fall away, my mind becomes quiet. Part of me is watching the quietness of my mind and enjoying it. I never knew I had this watching part before. It doesn't need to think. It's just there, aware of everything but separate from it—a wise old part of me.

That starts me wondering about Jane. How can she be seventy-seven and look younger than my grandma, who's sixty-one? Her skin is smooth, her eyes clear. She stands up straight, not at all hunched over. And she acts young.

I realize I'm off the mantra, drifting on thoughts, so I pick the sound up again and follow it as it gets fainter and finer. Then other thoughts rush in. I'm still mad at Jane for thinking I stole the money. For a while I just sit there feeling mad at her, then it gradually goes away.

The mantra comes back and I become the watcher again, not thinking, just observing. The mantra becomes more a pulsating light than a sound. It seems to light up something, a big cavern that's inside of me but also outside of me. The boundaries between me and everything else disappear—there's no difference now between inside and outside. I can see dimly into the cavern. The walls and ceiling are crystal, its facets glinting in the mantra light. Below them in all directions stretches a vast dark sea of water, its ripples gleaming. It's deep, deep as the earth, and I want to plunge in and dive all the way to the bottom. I'm sitting above it. Down there beneath me, beneath these rocks and dirt, rests the water.

I want to jump up and yell, "I found it!" but that thought makes it disappear. I take a deep breath and am back sitting cross-legged on my sleeping bag. Too stunned to say anything, I lie back and feel the ground under me, this good ground with all that good water under it.

I'm still lying there when Jane gets up. After a minute she comes over, looking concerned. "Are you all right?"

As I tell her about it, she sits down beside me and presses her hands to the earth, then grabs my hand and squeezes it. "You found it!"

"But how do we get it?"

She thinks a moment, finger to chin. "My plan was just to let people know about it, so they could use it. But we need to see if someone owns it. That could mess everything up."

We go into the Winnebago, and she turns on the computer, finds the phone number of the Shasta National Forest ranger station, and calls them on her cell phone. "Yes, hello. Can you tell me if the water rights in the national forest are still publicly owned, or have they been privatized?" She grimaces as she listens. "Oh, I see. Interesting. Well, thank you very much. Yes, you have a nice day too." She puts the phone down. "Damnit! The surface rights—the streams and lakes...what's left of them—are still public. But the government sold the subsurface rights for all the national forests five years ago to Chevron Aquatech. They're the only ones who can drill and pump water here. They'll just try to turn it into money. That's all they know."

"But we can't drill or tell anybody about it. How can we get it to the surface? " I ask.

"Don't know," Jane says. "But we might be able to figure that out if we get closer to it. All we have now is the general area."

"Maybe we could home in on it with one of those willow branches people use to find water."

"I'm afraid it's too dry here for willows," Jane says with a shake of her head. "They've become pretty much of a garden tree now...for people who can afford to water them."

"Hmm...."

"One possibility," Jane says. "Shasta is a live volcano. It hasn't erupted for hundreds of years, but it still gives off steam when the pressure builds up. And the steam comes out of vents, holes in the side of the mountain that are connected to the deeper shafts."

"You mean like a cave?"

"The vents themselves can be just cracks, but they lead deeper."

"How could we find them?"

"Good question." She stares off in thought. "Well...steam must be moist. Could be around the vents there's more vegetation growing. We could look for places that are greener."

"Dry as things are now, they should stand out. Let's take a hike and see what we can find," I say.

"First let's eat lunch."

"Good idea."

We make the food together in the tiny kitchen. Jane's vegetarian, and I'm getting bored with rice and tofu and cottage cheese, but with a can of beef enchiladas to go with it, it's OK.

Afterwards we hike up towards the lower slopes of the mountain. There are no trails here, but it's open enough that we can go cross country. It's slow going, though—climbing over rocks, circling around the big boulders, crunching through gravel. The rocks and even the sand are mostly black with glints of blue and green, and I can almost feel how they were formed deep in the blast furnace of the volcano and spewed out red hot.

We look for green patches but don't see any. Every couple of hundred yards we turn around to check our return route.

"We can't search all over," Jane says. "It's too huge, and I'm tired already. We need to tune our minds to the water and the steam vents. Don't concentrate on them, just feel connected to them and be open to what they're telling us."

I'm not sure how to do that, but I imagine myself as a drop of water that knows how to trickle down to the inner ocean, like the mantra flowing down to deeper levels and merging into the unified field. *Show me the path!*

We walk farther. I'm getting tired too. Ground squirrels scamper among the rocks, chattering warnings of our presence, and an eagle glides the thermal currents above us, probably hunting ground squirrels. No shade, and the sun glares down.

Jane is wearing a hat and sunglasses, but I don't have any. I'm thinking the mountain looks better from a distance than up close. But I can see why the Native Americans think Shasta is a holy being. It really seems to have a living presence, almost a personality, but very high and aloof, as if individual human beings aren't any more important to it than individual ground squirrels.

We come to a ravine that cuts into the slope. "Let's take a look in there," Jane says. Inside the notch the land flattens and becomes a rocky shelf. I can't see the peak from here because we're too far in. The view to the north, though, is grand—a flowing expanse of gray-green forested hills running to the horizon, probably in Oregon. Jane pulls a water bottle out of the small rucksack she's carrying, and we drink deeply. I picture the underground ocean of water deep beneath these dry rocks. *Lead me there*, I think to no one in particular.

My eyes fall on a sprig of purple lupin in the middle of a patch of moss. I walk closer and see a bit of green grass, not the brown I'm used to. It's two feet of meadow amid the dry rocks. A rabbit is nibbling the greenery. His ears perk up as he hears me, and he bounds away. The moss is at the point where two boulders meet; between them is a dark, narrow gap. I put my hand in it and feel warm air flowing out. I bend my head to it and smell dank mountain caverns, exhalations from the moist depths of the earth. I touch the moss like a shrine. *Thank you!*

"Lady Jane, would you look here?" I call to my companion.

After a hugging dance of jubilation, we trek back to the motor home, talking about ways we might reach the water. It could be impossible, at least without major equipment. This vent is too narrow to crawl into and the boulders are too big to push aside, but there's a chance the vent opens up into a larger shaft, and we might be able to dig down to it behind the boulders.

I want to try it. Even if I can't bring the water to the surface, I want to see it—those sparkling crystal caverns and the water so still and endless. I want more than just to see it—I want to drink some of that water, swim in it.

Getting down to it could be dangerous—we could be crushed underground or get arrested afterwards—but the rewards outweigh the risks. If we can get the water flowing, the whole world will change. If I die, well, everybody dies but not usually for a great cause. If we get arrested, well, Jane's been arrested before, and it hasn't hurt her. I know if I pass this up, I'll regret it the rest of my life.

That evening we meditate together and both have the same vision of the underground ocean and the caverns. Jane calls friends back in LA and tells them about the water. Afterwards she offers me the phone if I want to call home.

I don't want to talk to my parents and hear them try to convince me to come back. "Thanks, but no," I tell Jane. "Maybe I'll send them an email tomorrow."

We split the frozen pizza for dinner. Jane picks the pepperonis off her pieces and gives them to me. "I guess we've become a team," she says.

"Good." Her green eyes—what kind of green is it? Not emerald or turquoise. I know—I saw a movie once filmed in Jamaica. The sun was setting over the ocean and turned the sky around it orange and green. That's the green of her eyes— Jamaica sunset green.

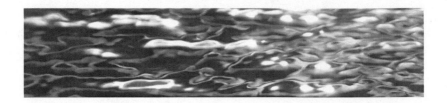

Next morning we drive back into Weed to buy equipment: pickax, shovel, buckets, and kneepads at the hardware store; forehead lamps, climbing rope, topographic map, more water canteens, and a hat for me at the sporting goods.

I buy the fuel pump for the bike. Jane offers to pay for it, but I don't want to always be sponging off her. Weed isn't big enough to have a discount parts store, so it costs ninety-eight dollars, a sizable chunk of my remaining cash.

Jane finds the approximate area of our steam vent on the topo map and a way to drive closer to it to save walking. We park there, load up the rucksack, and hike to our secret spot. Using the pickax and shovel, I try to pry the boulders at the steam vent apart, but they're too heavy. I don't want to dig under them because they might collapse, so I go behind them, clear away the rocks, and start hacking out a hole with the pickax. After a while the rocks give way to sand, and I can use the shovel—hard, hot work. I'm wearing the motorcycle gloves to prevent blisters, so my hands are sweating. I feel like a chain-gang laborer. If we get arrested, I might end up being one.

Jane is exploring the area for more vents. I'm in up to my thighs now, coughing from the dust I've raised, wondering if I've picked the wrong spot to dig. I jab the shovel in again, and it just keeps going. So do I. The ground collapses beneath me, and I fall through the hole with a scream, hitting my elbows on the sides, crashing down onto a rock floor ten feet below. A flash of pain shoots through my ankle. Dirt and stones pile down onto me. A flapping, skittering sound startles me; dark forms fly past my head—bats. I wince as one careens off my shoulder. Then they're gone, out the vent hole between the boulders. Their odor remains.

"Jane!" I cry. "Jane!" No response.

Then I hear a faint, "Bob?" The hole above me disappears, replaced by her silhouette. "Bob! Are you all right?"

"Not very."

"Anything broken?"

My ankle hurts but I can move it. "No. I think I'm OK. Just sore."

"I saw bats flying," Jane says. "Are you in a cave?"

"Not sure. It's a big hole."

"Can you climb out?"

"No, it's too big, too high. I need the rope."

Her silhouette disappears. I look around in the dim light from above. The rock floor slopes away down a narrow passage. The air wafting from there is fresher, smelling of water and stone.

The light disappears again as Jane leans over the hole. "I tied the rope around a boulder. Here's the other end."

I hear a slithering sound, then the coil striking the ground. When I pull on the rope, more dirt falls down on me, but it holds firmly. I try to climb it, pinching the rope between my feet, one on top of the other, while pulling up with my arms. The rope, though, is too thin to get a good grip—it slips between my feet, and the pressure hurts my ankle. Starting as high up as I can reach, I tie loops in it for my hands and feet. Then I climb up, dowsed with more falling dirt, and Jane helps me clamber back on the surface.

I tell her I'm going back down to find the water, and she insists on coming with me. As we're packing the gear, she sees me limping. "Oh, you're hurt."

"Twisted my ankle."

"Let's see it," she says, worried. I raise the leg, and she pulls the pants away from the ankle. "How bad is it?"

"Not too bad."

"It's starting to swell. Are you sure you can walk?"

I pace around a bit unsteadily. "It's bearable. I think it'll be OK. I've had worse from soccer."

"Tell me if it gets too bad. We'll both come back," she says.

I put on the rucksack, and we strap on the forehead lamps and climb into the hole. It's like being swallowed by a giant mouth into the earth's gullet. Our lamps cast weird bobbling shadows and let us see swarms of cockroaches and centipedes feasting on piles of bat shit. "Yuck!" says Jane, raising her hands in disgust. "I hope there's no snakes."

Carrying the pickax and shovel in my hands, I start down the narrow passage. "We're like two of Tolkien's hobbits on a spelunking expedition," Jane says from behind.

I don't know what this means, so she explains, which makes me want to read the books. The ceiling gets lower and lower, and I walk in a crouch after bumping my head a few times. The rock-and-dirt walls are dry and cool. Soon it's too low even to crouch. "We're going to have to crawl," I tell Jane, "or give up."

"Then we crawl," she replies and drops to her knees.

I take off the pack, take out kneepads for both of us, and strap the pickax and shovel to the pack. Holding the pack in front of me, I crawl on my knees. The kneepads help—a little. The space gets more cramped, and I have to lie on my belly and push with my feet while shoving the pack ahead. It's awkward, slow, painful. Each push hurts my ankle. I start feeling claustrophobic, breathing in short rapid gasps, imagining the walls caving in, trapped, unable to move, slowly dying.

"Let's stop for a minute," Jane says. "Just lie here and meditate. It'll calm us down."

I think she means me and not us. She sounds fine, but I can't even talk I'm so scared. If I opened my mouth, I'd scream. I want out! But if this seventy-seven-year-old lady can handle it, why can't I? I don't want to seem like a coward when she's so brave. I close my eyes and think my mantra. At first it's as fast and fluttery as my breath and heart, but then it slows, and my body follows it, gradually calming. After a few minutes I'm ready to start again.

I push the pack and crawl farther down the tunnel. I'm banging my head, elbows, and knees on the rocks, and Jane's little yelps of pain tell me she's doing the same. If it gets any tighter, we'll have to leave. And backing out of this squeeze would be even harder than crawling in.

But then the floor drops a bit, and I can rise to my hands and knees. The space increases into a sort of wedge, and we can gradually stand up. I put the pack on. As the floor continues to descend, it gets moist. "Water! Maybe we're getting close."

"I hope so. I've had enough adventure," Jane says. "But it could be just a spring."

Soon we're sloshing through water, then it's over our knees, up to our waists. Cold. "How can we tell if this is really it?" I ask.

"I don't know. Let's try to keep going."

By the time it's up to my chest, Jane says, "I'm swimming. If it looks like our lamps might get wet, we need to turn around."

"Yeah, definitely don't want to be in the dark down here. And I don't think I can swim with this pack."

The floor takes a dip, and I'm dog-paddling, the handles of the pickax and shovel wobbling above my head. Part of me is screaming to turn around, but another part wants to keep going. After several lunging breaststrokes, my foot strikes solid ground. Gradually the floor ascends, and I slog forward.

"Walking again!" says Jane.

The shaft rises totally out of the water. We're soaked, but the ground beneath us is dry. We climb farther, and at the peak of the incline I pause to rest. Jane comes up beside me, breathing hard. From here the shaft drops steeply and disappears around a bend. We give each other silent, exhausted looks that ask, *Do we really want to do this?* We nod and move on.

The steepness of the decline makes us hold to the rocky sides to keep from pitching forward. Around the bend the passage opens out above us. The beams of our lamps dart and waver, falling first on the rising ceiling, then on the walls expanding into an amphitheater, and finally on the floor, which is no floor at all but a glinting, shimmering surface of water stretching out an endless distance ahead. From the ceiling condensed drops are falling with little plinks and plops and plunks, rippling the surface into intermeshing concentric rings. The damp rocks of the ceiling sparkle like crystal.

"This is what I saw in meditation," Jane says.

"Me too!"

The air smells as fresh as all the rains of spring that used to be and now may be again. I grab Jane and give her a big kiss on the cheek. My wavering beam shows her startled face. Holding hands, we look out over water…water…water…until our lamplights disappear in the distance.

"I want to taste it." Jane stoops down and scoops some up in her hand. "Delicious!"

I drink some too—totally refreshing, not at all stagnant, although it must have been here a long time. "I want to dive in," I say.

"Brrr…too cold for me. But let's meditate here."

We sit on the rocks, which are damp and slick from the dripping water. We're already so wet, though, that it doesn't bother us. "Let's turn off our lamps to save the batteries," Jane says. We do, but suddenly it's pitch dark. I can't see anything. It's as if the ground has disappeared with the light and left me floating. The drops sound louder now. "No, that's too spooky," she says and turns hers back on. "You can leave yours off."

I close my eyes, but it's still not as dark as it was with my eyes open and lamps off. It's chilly, though, and drops sometimes fall on my head. Despite that, the mantra takes me away from thoughts to that boundless place where my mind becomes a vast pool connected to everything. My everyday self disappears and I merge with something infinite, timeless. I can flow everywhere by not thinking, just being there and observing, a sense of thoughtless knowing. I'm a great sea of consciousness like this water.

I can sense the sea's immensity, stretching from California under the Great Basin of Nevada, Utah, and Arizona, this parched American desert, the last place the deep drillers would've looked. We're sitting by the tip of it closest to the surface. From here it goes deeper and deeper, soaking through strata of sand and porous rock, a huge aquifer waiting to be freed and flow again.

"We did it," Jane whispers. "This is it." We come out of meditation, leaving our inner ocean, and sit side by side looking out at the subterranean ocean. "I've never seen anything so beautiful," she whispers.

Coming back to the surface is less scary than going in—we know what to expect. The sudden light as we climb out of the shaft, though, is a shock.

Jane squints, stretches her arms, and says, "Have to tell my friends back home." She takes out her cell phone and punches buttons. "Naomi—Jane. Great news! We just found the Saudi Arabia of water." She describes it while I haul the rope back up and get ready to leave.

The walk down is also easier than it was going up, despite pain in my ankle. We stroll along light headed with triumph. A gravel slope that we had to laboriously struggle up we can now glide down in our shoes, skiing through the scree, pushing pebbles out of the way and sending them rolling, bouncing, and clattering down the slope. We almost fall but manage to stay on our feet. Finally we enter the forest, its cool, late afternoon shadows a welcome relief from the bright, bare volcanic rocks.

"Now comes the next problem," Jane says. "How do we keep Chevron from grabbing it? To them it's just another commodity. They'll hold it off the market to drive up the price until people are desperate. They don't care. They're just a machine run by corporate robots who are programmed to do only one thing—get money. Somehow we have to bring it to the surface, where it's public."

"That's a lot of water to get to the surface," I say.

"We just need to get it flowing. Then it'll run down the mountain and fill the Sacramento River, and from there it'll water the whole Central Valley. It'll evaporate and form clouds, then rain back down on us. The land will become damp and fertile again. Crops will grow. It'll turn the balance back toward moist, flourishing life and away from dry, wilting death."

She's really inspired me to do whatever I can to make this happen. The water here is already so close to the surface, there has to be some way to get it moving. "Maybe with a siphon," I tell her. "Run some kind of big hose down there and start a vacuum that would suck the water out, and then it would flow by itself."

"Hmm...but that's still pumping it out. It's a man-made way of getting it to the surface, and Chevron could stop it. The only thing they couldn't stop would be a natural process, something from inside the earth that makes the water run out."

"If the ceiling could cave in...."

"We can't blow up the mountain," Jane says.

"How about...look, we got down there through a vent shaft. And there must be others. Maybe we can find one lower down, below the water level, one where the exit is stopped up so the water can't get out. Then if we broke an opening in it, the water would run out from its own pressure."

"But how would we find that, especially if it's covered over?" she asks.

"From the inside. I'd scuba down with a light and look for shafts under water, tunnels where the water runs back in. If the shaft goes close enough to the surface of the mountain, I can dig through underwater with the pickax. I might have to dig a couple of hours a day for a few days, but it could work."

"It sounds so risky," Jane objects.

"I'll be careful. If it doesn't look possible, I won't force it. I'll just come back."

Jane grimaces. "Let's try to think of another way."

We walk along in silence awhile, and I'm struck by how birdlike she is—small but very bright and alert. Her eyes are wide open to take everything in. And she's quick, not so much in her movements but in her thoughts, the way she explains things. What kind of a bird? I think a robin. And now she's trying to pull this great worm of water out of the earth.

"It'd be terrible if you got hurt down there because of my scheme," she says. "I'd never forgive myself."

"This part is my scheme. I've always wanted to have an adventure. But I'll be careful."

"Well...OK. Don't do anything risky."

By now we can see the Winnebago. Suddenly I'm hungry and exhausted.

Jane must be too. "How about an adventurous dinner of canned ravioli? Beef for you and cheese for me," she says.

"Good."

In addition to the main course, Jane insists on cooking a bunch of vegetables. I insist on brownies for dessert. We eat in the dining nook across from the kitchen, little but cozy. Since Jane cooked, I do the dishes (one thing the motor home doesn't have is a dishwasher).

She cleans my rucksack and mends the rip in it. "Bob, if you're sure you want to do this, go ahead. I'll help as much as I can, which unfortunately won't be very much. But you'll need scuba gear."

"We can get that at the sporting goods store."

"Well, the least I can do is pay for it."

"OK, thanks. We'll get it tomorrow."

"There's another problem, though," Jane says. "We may get into trouble if you pitch your tent here. It's illegal to camp anywhere except the official places, and they're over on the other side, about an hour's drive. If a ranger sees your tent here, you'll get a ticket, and it may make them suspicious about what else we're doing. We're not even supposed to be off the marked trails. Hiking cross country is against the rules...and so is the digging.

"So they don't notice us as much, how about if you sleep on the couch tonight? And we'll move the RV so it's not as noticeable."

"Sure, good idea."

She drives to a more secluded place where we can pull farther off the road. As she's making up the couch for me, I start thinking: Maybe she has something else in mind with the couch. Maybe she might like to.... I know I would. I would love to hold her and touch her. She's really very pretty. She's a bit skinny but still has a nice shape. Her breasts and hips are curvy, and her skin is smooth, hardly wrinkled. But it's more than just the way she looks. I really like her. I'd like to kiss her and hold her and be close to her. And then.... Yes, I'd really like to do that too.

I step behind her, put my hands on her hips, nuzzle my nose through her long gray hair, and kiss her on the back of the neck.

She stiffens. "Bob! What are you doing?"

"Kissing you."

She turns around, and I put my hands on her shoulders and kiss her on the lips. She stands still a moment, then backs away, her large green eyes now round. "Bob! Where did you get that idea?"

"A little bird told me."

"Tell that little bird to fly away!"

I want to kiss her again, but I'm afraid she'll get mad. "I just thought...maybe we could...."

She puts her hands on her hips. "You want to jump these old bones? No!"

"But...."

"No butts—especially not mine!" Then she laughs. "Bob,

really, we can't do this. I'm old enough to be your grandmother."

Now I'm feeling mean, so I want to tell her she's a lot older than my grandmother.

"I like you...very much. I really care about you. But not in that way. I'm too old for that." She turns up the palms of her hands.

"Well, OK. I'm sorry I tried."

"Don't be sorry. I'm flattered. It's just that...." Her hands nervously stir the air.

"What?"

"It wouldn't be right. You should find a girl your own age."

I get mad because she's making me feel like a kid. "What does age have to do with it? I thought you were a radical, but you're sounding like some advice columnist."

She looked at me with a mix of pity and surprise. "You dear boy...oops, sorry, I mean man. You really are attracted to me, aren't you?"

"That's OK, we can forget about it."

"Well, this is not the kind of thing one can forget, but we don't need to *do it*. It's nice that you would think of me in that way. But really...." She shakes her head.

"OK, I'll be good." I turn away in disappointment, not realizing how much I wanted her until she turned me down.

"Now your feelings are hurt," she says. "I don't know what to do. Will you still be my friend?"

I glance back at her. With the pleading expression on her face, she looks even prettier. "Definitely," I say.

"Good. Thank you." She extends her hand for a conciliatory shake.

I take it. It's warm and soft. I can't help staring at her breasts rising and falling as she breathes...heavily.

"Please don't be offended," she says.

By now I just want to drop the topic. "It's OK. I don't blame you. It was a dumb idea."

"If you need another blanket, they're up here on the shelf."

"I won't."

"Well...sleep well. And we'll talk more in the morning."

We both give the other a little embarrassed wave, and Jane goes into her bedroom. I can hear the little click of the latch to lock her door. This makes me even madder. Did she think I would come in and rape her?

It's a long time before I can fall asleep. I keep thinking about her, sometimes mad at her, sometimes wanting her, sometimes both together.

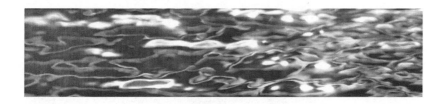

At breakfast Jane is busily cheery. OK, she doesn't want to talk about it. That's fine with me. Instead we talk about diving. She's never done it, so I tell her how great it is. When I worked as a helper at the scuba school, we used to dive off Catalina, where there's some coral. I love the silent beauty of this other world. We talk about the equipment I'll need. I have all the gear at home, but that doesn't do us much good here.

After breakfast we take a walk through the woods. As we come to a clearing, motion on the other side catches my eye. Out of the trees steps a black-tailed doe. She sees us and pauses, one foot raised, sniffing, listening, looking. Jane and I stare enthralled. As the doe gazes at us, our eyes join across the space, across the species. Communication flows between us: cautious curiosity about a fellow creature. She breaks contact, begins nibbling dry grass, then looks back at us as if saying, *As long as you stay on your side, it's OK.*

We watch her in delight, then turn away and leave the clearing to her.

The sporting goods store in Weed has a small selection of overpriced scuba gear, for sale only, no rentals. It's not the best gear, but I find everything I need. Getting all this stuff is like Christmas.

As we're driving back, a helicopter passes over us, then returns and stays above us, like a buzzing fly. It's whomp-whomp noise is annoying. "That's enough to make you paranoid," Jane says.

Flashing lights fill the mirrors. A police car comes up fast behind us and turns on its siren. "Not paranoid, it's true," Jane says, pulling off to the side.

"Stand out of the vehicle," the loudspeaker on the car orders. "Extend your arms and legs and lean against the side of the vehicle."

"This is bad," Jane says. "Whatever it's about, don't tell them anything. Just say I'm your lawyer and you have the right to discuss the case with me."

We obey the loudspeaker command. When we're standing and leaning against the Winnebago as if we're trying to push it over, two cops get out of the car, one with his pistol drawn. They approach wordlessly, and the one with his pistol still holstered pats us all over our bodies. He smells of cigarettes and coffee. The other one stands guard, pistol in hand but not pointed at us.

"What is this about?" Jane demands.

The cop ignores her. When he finishes searching us, he says, "See your IDs."

I give him my driver's license. He looks at the picture, then at me, and puts it in his pocket.

Jane says, "Mine's inside."

"I'll go with you," the cop with his pistol drawn says. They go into the motor home, then come out with the cop holding her license and keys.

"What's this about?" Jane asks again.

"You're both under arrest," her cop says. He pulls a card from his pocket and reads us our rights.

"Do you have a warrant?" she asks.

"We have a warrant to arrest both of you and search your premises."

"Let me see the warrant."

"Turn around and put your hands behind your back," he orders and takes handcuffs from his belt.

"I have a right to see the warrant!" she insists.

"You can see it at the courthouse. If you don't submit to handcuffing, I'll do it forcibly."

Jane turns around and puts her hands behind her back. Cords are standing out on her neck.

"You too," my cop tells me. I obey, and the slap of plastic handcuffs stings my wrists.

"Get in the back of the car," Jane's cop tell us. "My partner will follow us in your vehicle."

The back of the car is separated from the front by wire mesh. "Where are you taking us?" Jane asks.

"County jail in Yreka."

Jane and I exchange forlorn glances. "Meditate," she says and closes her eyes.

Fat chance that helping, I think. But it does. At first my mind is filled with fear—*What are these bastards going to do to us?*—but gradually the mantra eases them away, and I feel calmer. Whatever it is, they're not likely to shoot us. We'll get over it. I don't have a real peaceful meditation—the police radio is blaring, the handcuffs are digging into my back, I'm still angry and afraid, but all that isn't overwhelming me. I've got some distance on it.

The cop parks by the sheriff's office in back of the courthouse, and the Winnebago pulls in on the other side. The cop unlocks our door, opens it, and gestures us to get out. That's hard with our hands cuffed behind our backs—no way to grip anything. I stumble but manage to stay on my feet, but Jane falls onto the asphalt. I try to help her up but can't. Then the cop grips her under both arms and lifts her onto her feet. I guess he thinks he's being chivalrous.

Inside they take the cuffs off, fingerprint us, photograph us, then take us into separate rooms for a strip search. A guard, stocky with a short neck, looks in my mouth and sticks a finger in my ass to see if I have weapons or drugs. Poor Jane—she has to go through this too, or worse. I get my clothes back, but every-thing's been taken out of the pockets. I thought I'd have to wear jail clothes. But maybe that's just for prison. And we're not there...yet.

After I sign a paper with a list of everything that was in my pockets, the guard takes me down the hall into an office where a man in a brown sport coat and knit tie is sitting behind a desk. "Have a seat," he says, motioning to a chair in front of his desk. I sit down, and the guard steps back against the wall. The man has a crew cut and looks like he was a football player ten years and fifty pounds ago. He shrugs in a friendly way. "So you messed up and you're in trouble. You got a clean record so far, but the last thing a young guy just starting out in life needs is a prison record. An arrest record is one thing, but a prison record puts you into the lowest category for any kind of job. About all you can do is go into the military. And even they may not take you." He gestures to the papers on his desk. "What you got here could mean prison, but it doesn't have to. We got a certain leeway with this kind of stuff. You want to stay out of prison?"

"Yes."

"Good. You've heard the stories. The reality is even worse. Especially for a young, good-looking guy like you. Those old cons will tear you apart.

"We can keep you out of there. You plead guilty to this stuff here"—gesturing again at the papers—"we'll let you off with a $500 fine. No jail time. You'll be out of here as soon as you pay the fine." He pushes a paper and pen across the desk to me. "Take my advice. Read this and sign it. Otherwise we're going to have to play hardball, and you'll end up in prison."

He's got me scared. I really want to sign the paper—the easy way out. I'm pretty sure my folks would wire the money for the fine. I'd have to go back home and get a shit job to pay for it, but I'd stay out of prison. But Jane told me not to make any statements. Plus he could be bluffing me. I might not go to prison anyway. How much evidence could they have on us? The phone call and a hole in the ground. They didn't catch us actually drilling or pumping water. I take a deep breath and say, "No, I'm not going to sign it."

Scowling, he pulls the paper back. "OK, it's your life. Don't say I didn't warn you."

"Jane is my attorney. When can I meet with her?"

"You'll see her at the arraignment."

"When is that?"

"Some time in the next forty-eight hours. I'll give you another chance. If you change your mind after being locked up in the cell, and you don't want to live that way for a long time, you can plead guilty at the arraignment, and the deal will still hold."

"I'll keep it in mind."

He taps impatiently on the desk. "This is not high school anymore. This is the real world. And you better wise up, if you want to have any kind of future." He gestures to the guard, who moves towards me.

We go down another aqua-painted hall, this one dirty with scuff marks, to the cells. With an electronic gadget he opens the sliding metal door to one of them and puts me in with five other prisoners. "New guy," he tells them.

Three double-deck bunks, an open toilet and sink in the corner, and about ten feet of floor to pace around in. Most of the guys are sitting or lying on their bunks. One of them asks me what I'm in for, and I say, "Looking for water." They shrug, unimpressed.

A tall, skinny guy with short blond hair, long sideburns, and a droopy mustache says, "We had a water wildcatter in here couple of weeks ago. He got six months in Vacaville. Second offense. How many offenses you got?"

"First one."

"Then you'll walk. If you can pay the fine."

He's in for shoplifting, two of the others for growing marijuana, one for drunk and disorderly, and one for bad checks. There are three other cells like ours, mostly full. They let us out for meals and recreation. The meals are all packaged, like what you get on an airplane, but worse. The recreation is a wall-mounted TV, a ping-pong table, a card table, and an outdoor basketball court topped with barbed wire. What we mostly do is sit and stare into space. Lights are dimmed at ten p.m. I lie in my top bunk a long time wondering how Jane is doing.

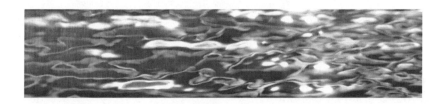

Loudspeaker wakes me: "Good morning, residents. Six a.m. Time to rise and shine." It takes me a moment to realize where I am, then the monotony begins again—empty time filled with noise, useless games, futile conversation. The prisoners who have to spend years, their whole lives, in these chicken-coop cages—what that must do to them, watching their lives drain away, helpless, hopeless. If they do get out, it's only into another prison of poverty and slums where the only escape is erasing themselves with drugs and ending up back here. Trapped. It's a wonder they don't kill everyone they see.

I'm lucky. I'll be out of here before long. But then I think, when I do get out, I'll have a record, and that'll make it harder for me to get even the shit jobs that are out there. And if I get desperate for money and break another law and get caught at it, I'll be in for a lot longer—repeat offender. Have even more trouble getting a job. If I have a family and see my kids ragged and hungry and the only way to help them is to steal something, I'd probably do it.

The few people at the top getting richer and richer. Now even the water belongs to them, what's left of it. Their hands hold the levers of power, running the politicians, the media, the armies, the cops, the courts. I never put all this together before, but here in jail it becomes clear.

I bat the ping-pong ball, I watch the game show, I shuffle the cards. Then I think, *Hey, my body has to be here, but my mind doesn't. I'll meditate.* I go into the cell and sit up on my bunk. The TV is blaring, men are talking and arguing, the ping-pong ball is pinging and ponging, but I start the mantra anyway and follow

71

it down as it gets fainter and smaller and my thoughts fall away and the noise fades into the background. One guy asks me what I'm doing, and I open one eye and say "Meditating," and he goes away. I sit there for about an hour, get up and stretch and walk around, then sit back down.

After a few hours of meditation, I feel outside of time. It's like all this is a play I'm watching from backstage. I'm the author of the play sitting in the wings watching myself and others act in it. Out there on the stage there's time—beginnings, middles, ends. But backstage there is no time. Everything just is.

"Parks!" someone barks at me. I open my eyes. It's my lower bunkmate, a burly Native-American in for bad checks. "Your butt's going to get sore just sitting there for hours. It's yard time. Let's go play some basketball."

He's right—it is sore. I could use some exercise.

As I'm running, dribbling, and shooting, I know that behind all this, backstage, I'm sitting there watching a play I wrote. Two different mes and two different levels of life—the busy, active surface and the still, quiet depths. Like the ocean. Meditation is like diving down to explore the depths and getting to know the other me who lives down there.

That night I dream about Jane. She's wearing a long nightgown and sinking into a pool of water. I'm trying to save her but all I'm wearing is a life jacket, and that holds me on the surface so I can't get to her. She smiles at me, and I grab for her hand, but it slips away and she goes down. I wake up with my heart pounding, the snores, snorts, and sighs of my fellow prisoners telling me I'm in jail.

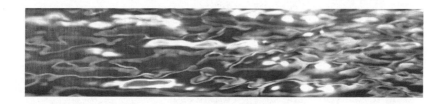

Breakfast is watery coffee, a mushy apple, and a plastic tray of scrambled eggs, sausage, and toast fresh out of the freezer and microwave. I wonder how Jane is doing with the food. Every meal has meat, so she's probably pretty hungry by now. But maybe she trades hers for more veggies.

After watching the morning news—USA and China exchanging threats, radiation leaks in the new atomic water desalination plant, crop failures driving the prices of food higher; sports: the Giants win, the Angels lose; weather: hot and sunny—I'm definitely ready to meditate. But just as I'm settling in, two guards come in with mops, brooms, and buckets. "Time to swamp down the cells. We're going to inspect afterwards, and they better be clean or else we'll cut back on your rec time."

The other guys know what to do, so I follow along—dusting shelves and windowsills, sweeping then mopping the concrete floor, everybody barefoot so we don't leave dirty tracks on it. The we do the same in the rec room. Takes hours. Two guys, black and white, from another cell get in a fight, and the guards beat them with clubs and haul them out into solitary. *Not much is being learned here*, I think.

Just as we're finishing, another guard comes in and asks, "Who's Parks?"

I raise my hand.

"Your arraignment. Let's go."

He handcuffs me, but this time with my hands in front, which doesn't hurt as much. We walk from the jail section over to the court section, where the walls are beige instead of aqua and the floors carpeted instead of linoleum.

Jane is already in the room, also cuffed, and we both smile in relief at seeing the other. The guard tells me to sit down beside her at the table. She has several sheets of paper in front of her and is leafing through them, awkwardly because of the handcuffs. "Good to see you," she says. "How was it?"

"Could've been worse," I answer.

"It may get worse. Let me speak for both of us, OK?"

"Good. You're the pro."

Ten feet away a man in a suit is sitting at another table like ours. In front of us on a raised platform is the judge's station, empty, with the flags of the USA and California standing behind it. The polished wooden door between the flags opens, and a woman in a black robe walks in. "All rise," says a guard. "The United States District Court for the Central District of California is in session, Magistrate Judge Laura Garcia presiding."

We stand up.

"Please be seated," the judge says as she takes her seat above us. She glances at papers and says, "This is the initial appearance in the case of the United States versus Jane Catherine Willoughby and Robert Christopher Parks. Are those your correct names?"

"Yes, Your Honor," says Jane.

I nod, not wanting to say anything. The judge stares at me and says, "Mr. Parks?"

"Yes, Your Honor."

She turns to Jane. "Ms. Willoughby, is my information correct that you are an attorney admitted to the bar of the State of California and that you are representing yourself and Mr. Parks?"

"Yes, Your Honor."

"You are both charged with attempted felony larceny on or about June 19, 2026 in Shasta National Forest by violating the property rights of a California corporation, Chevron Aquatech, to wit, by attempting to deprive them of their subsurface water rights. You are both further charged with misdemeanor damaging the natural landscape of the Shasta National Forest by digging and misdemeanor departing from the designated trails within the Shasta National Forest.

"The United States Attorney has informed me that if you enter pleas of guilty to all charges and agree to immediately leave Siskiyou County and not return for a period of one year, he will request the court to suspend all penalties."

I brighten. *Good! No fines! We can get out of here.*

"How do you plead, Ms. Willoughby?"

"Not guilty on all charges, Your Honor."

Oh no!

"Ms. Willoughby, I must inform you that a felony conviction may result in your being disbarred from the practice of law."

"I'll stand by my plea, Your Honor."

"Very well. And you Mr. Parks?"

I swallow and say, "Not guilty on all charges, Your Honor."

"Your Honor," Jane says, "I'm certain we can settle this case without going to trial. The US Attorney knows his evidence was obtained through electronic surveillance without a court order and is therefore not admissible. He's willing to waive penalties if we plead guilty because he has no case."

The judge turns to the man at the other table. "Mr. Flanagan, would you care to comment?"

The US attorney—tall with curly red hair, freckles, and blue eyes under horn-rimmed glasses—clears his throat and says, "We definitely have a case against the defendants."

The judge asks, "Did you employ electronic surveillance without a court order to get it?"

Flanagan keeps his mouth shut but twists it. Then he says, "The source of our information could be discussed at the trial."

"There's not going to be a trial, Mr. Flanagan, if your evidence was obtained without a court order. We can save the taxpayers of the State of California the expense of a trial."

"I request we speak in chambers, Your Honor," says the US attorney.

She frowns and says, "Considering this is just an initial appearance, I'll grant your request. Court is in recess for ten minutes."

Garcia and Flanagan leave through the door between the flags.

Jane smiles.

"What's going on?" I ask her.

"I took a chance, but it looks like I'm right," she whispers. "The only way they could've known we found the water was if they were monitoring my phone calls."

"How would they know your number, though?"

"Easy. Your ex-boss got us put on the suspect list with a description of the RV and the license plate. Based on that, the highway patrol stops us the first time and gets our IDs. Then it's no problem to get the cell phone number and snoop with electronic scanners."

"Why would the police care so much to do that?" I ask.

"It's not the police. It's Chevron, it's the corporations. They care. And they have a lot of influence in the government. They don't totally control it yet, but they have power in parts of it."

"But why isn't it admissible as evidence?"

"I don't think the cops had time to get a court order for the surveillance. It was too quick. There are so many people on the suspect list the cops usually don't get a court order until they're sure something's going on. But when they knew we'd already found the water, they had to move fast, before we got it flowing to the surface. So they busted us."

"Can we get off?"

"We'll see."

The judge returns looking peeved; the US attorney follows looking scolded. The judge pounds her gavel. "Court is dismissing all charges against the defendants."

"Your Honor," Flanagan says, "we request that this dismissal not affect the search warrant for their vehicle. That may yield further evidence. Ms. Willoughby is, after all, a repeat offender."

"Request granted," the judge says. "I'm releasing the defendants on their own recognizance pending inspection of their vehicle."

"Objection, Your Honor," Jane says. "The sheriff has had forty-eight hours to search our vehicle."

Flanagan shakes his head. "The sheriff's office has been extremely busy, and they haven't yet had time to thoroughly search it. The vehicle in question is a large RV of the type often used for drug transport."

"When can the search be completed?" the judge asks.

"Definitely by this evening," Flanagan says.

"In that case I'll overrule the objection," the judge says. "The vehicle remains impounded pending completion of the search, provided that is completed today." She bangs her gavel. "Court is hereby adjourned."

Flanagan speaks to us without looking at us. "The bailiff will arrange your release. And a deputy will notify you by cell phone when the vehicle search is completed."

"Obviously you already have the number. When will that be?" Jane says.

He looks down at her with a half smile. "Hard to say. You'll have to ask the sheriff's office."

The bailiff takes us downstairs to the sheriff's office, and Jane asks the deputy at the desk when we can get the motor home back.

"That's up to the evening shift," the man says. "We had too much to do today to get around to it. I'll mark it priority for them. Keep your phone on, and they'll call you when it's done."

"What are we supposed to do in the meantime?"

"Whatever you want. You're released, but you're still under charges. If anything criminal is found in your vehicle, you'll be taken back into custody. For now you're free to go." He gives us two bags containing our personal items and some forms to sign.

We leave and stroll around downtown Yreka, which takes about fifteen minutes, then sit through a movie double feature— a sad love story and a comedy about the end of the world.

"Time to meditate," Jane says. We find a park with a few trees and sit on a bench. Cars are driving by, children are laughing and chattering as they play on the sliding board, jungle gym, and teeter-totter nearby, and a breeze keeps teasing my mind away from the mantra, but despite that I settle in to an inner quietness. The mantra gets fainter until it's just a wisp of sound.

I can see the water now, at first dimly, then more clearly, stretching out to what seems infinity, rippling with drops falling from the glistening ceiling. This cavern is deep in the earth, but that's just the surface of the water. I need to go to its depths and find a way to make it flow.

My mind clings to the mantra. Each time it gets fainter, I go deeper into the water—it's like a diving bell taking me down. I'm barely breathing. I can see the rocks of the bottom—glowing. I feel their warmth. At first it's pleasant, then it gets too hot.

Maybe I'm going into hell!

The water and rocks disappear, and I'm back on the park bench, breathing rapidly, heart racing. *Hell is a vicious fantasy invented to control people through fear,* I tell myself. *Put it out of your mind.* I start the mantra again and gradually calm down. My mind is empty now, no visions. Even the mantra disappears. I seem to expand out in all directions and leave behind the small self, the little me. It's like breaking out of a prison, shedding a cocoon, or pecking through an eggshell. I'm huge now, free. This self, the big me, has been here the whole time, watching the little me.

"Slowly let's open our eyes," Jane says.

When I do, the park seems different. The noise of the kids had bothered me before, but now it's almost like music. They're radiating so much fresh energy as they tear around, totally wrapped up in their play. The adults too have an inner light, but it's covered by sadness and tiredness. It's like there are two levels going on, deeper joy hidden under surface suffering. Meditation can bring the deeper level to the surface, like we're trying to do with the water.

The tower of the courthouse looms above us from a block away, one of those institutions designed to block the joy. "I think Flanagan is lying about the sheriff not having time to search the Winnebago," Jane says. "And they delayed the arraignment as long as they could, the full forty-eight hours. For some reason they don't want to let us go."

"What if they plant something in the Winnebago, drugs or something so they could really send us up?" I ask.

"Not likely," she replies. "They might do that for a major crime, if they really wanted to get us, but we're too minor league for that. I don't think they'd go that far.

"But now you've got an arrest record. Welcome to the club. Anybody who really resists gets arrested these days. But not resisting means serving the system, being a collaborator."

That makes me feel better about breaking the law. Our crime helps people and hurts a corporation.

We eat dinner in a Chinese restaurant. As we're polishing off the lychee nuts about eight p.m., Jane's cell phone jingles: No incriminating evidence found in the vehicle. We can drive it away.

We do.

"They'll be watching us now," Jane says as she drives. "And they know where to look. Only one way they could've known we were digging—they must've pinpointed the place where I made the phone call and then gone there. Now they know we're trying to get the water to the surface where it's not going to be theirs anymore. They'll go after it as soon as they can."

"Then let's try tonight," I say. "Might be our last chance."

"Are you up for that?"

"Definitely. I may need some coffee though."

"I'll make it right now."

We park as close to our trail as we can get, and I load the gear into the pack, strapping the pickax to the outside. It's heavy, like when I packed up to leave.

We hike out of the forest into the rocky, open terrain leading up to the mountain. A wafer of moon casts silvery light over Shasta's steep slopes. An owl flies by with a whoosh, turns in mid air, and plunges to earth. After a flapping of wings the bird lofts again, clutching a small, limp form in its talons.

Jane shudders. "Poor little thing. I've never liked that our culture glorifies the predator. The people with real power in our society, the CEOs, are predatory personalities. That's how they got there. They embody the values of the system—dog-eat-dog competition to hoard economic resources. They exploit their employees and destroy their rivals, all to get richer. And they become the models for the rest of us. We're supposed to identify with the predators—the owls, the hawks, the lions, the wolves. Get out there and fight. Life is a battle. Be a winner.

"But life doesn't have to be a battle. There's enough for everyone. But not enough for people to grab a huge share and get rich.

"There's enough water for everyone too, if we can get it flowing again. But not if Chevron gets it."

We trudge up the scree slope we had skied down three days ago, then cut across a plateau towards the site. From a distance, though, we can see it's changed. A square shape intrudes on the landscape.

"Uh oh," Jane says, "they've started already."

"Damn!"

A strip of yellow-and-black plastic tape attached to metal poles surrounds the site. From the poles hang signs:

No Trespassing under Penalty of Law!
Chevron Aquatech
Leaders in Deep-Drilling Water Technology

Behind the tape are a square stack of metal forms and piles of rods, brackets, other hardware.

"They've claimed it," Jane says with disgust. "Building a platform to drill on. Must've brought all this in by helicopter."

"Should we go under the tape?" I ask.

"Yes."

I lift it so she can go under.

"No, wait," she says. "Let's not bend for these bastards." She takes out her pocket knife and slashes through the tape. "There, Mr. Chevron!" She turns to me with a bow and an inviting flourish. "After you, Mr. Parks."

We stroll across the barrier and make our way through the stacks of metal. The ground around them is barer than it was before. The helicopter wind must've blown away the sand. The hole I dug is now circled with spray-painted markings.

I start to get scared. I might never get back to the surface—trapped down there, crushed, or drowned. But I could never live with myself if I didn't take the chance. We can't let them grab up all the water. And why stay in a world that's becoming a desert?

Jane must be nervous too because she asks, "Bob, are you sure you want to do this?"

Something about the way she asks makes me want to do it even more. I nod. "Yeah, I am." *Really?* I ask myself.

She touches my hand. "I would hate to lose you."

"Thanks. Me too. It's a risk, but if we can free the water, it's worth it. I'll be careful. If it doesn't look like it's going to work, I won't push it. I'll leave—promise. I don't have a death wish."

"Good." She keeps her hand on mine and looks at me. "We've become friends...gone through some difficult times together...some misunderstandings...but I'm very happy you joined up with me. You've really made it possible for us to get this far."

"I like it too. That's why we can't quit now."

She squeezes my hand. "What can I do to help?"

"Stay up here and make sure no one takes away the rope!"

She hugs me but tries not to do it full on, so I don't get ideas again. "You're very brave, Bob." She laughs nervously. "You make me wish I were fifty years younger."

I start getting ideas again. "I better get down there."

We run the rope through the pack frame and lower it into the hole, then fasten the rope around the boulders. I click on my head lamp and climb down, using the loops as a ladder.

The bats are gone, out working the night shift, but the cockroaches and centipedes are still at home. I put the pack on and creep down the narrow shaft, more scared now being alone. At least it's a familiar route. I try to think of other positives, to ward off the fear. My ankle doesn't hurt anymore. This is a real adventure, better than any movie. I imagine all the water flowing out and filling the rivers and lakes and irrigating the fields, evaporating and raining back down. I think how wonderful rain is. If I die, I'll just evaporate up, wait awhile, and come back down again. I'm part of the cycle too. Everything is part of this huge pool of energy that's forever taking on different forms. The forms come and go, but we're the energy, not the form.

If I'd just heard this as an idea, it wouldn't mean much. But meditating and bringing my mind down into the unified field, letting all the boundaries dissolve and becoming one with it, but still staying myself, I know I *am* it—I'm as infinite and eternal as it is.

All this gets rid of about two-thirds of my fear. The rest is still there, sulking in the background.

The shaft drops down into the flooded section, and when the head space gets too small, I take off the pack, hold it in front of me, and walk bent over. But there's more water in the shaft now.

Up ahead it's totally flooded—no room to breathe, and my lamp would go out.

I turn around and slosh back out. Although the passage is narrow, I manage to unpack the scuba gear and put it on: wet suit, BC vest, tanks, regulator, weight belt, fins, and mask. I exchange my camping head lamp for the waterproof diving lamp.

Leaving the pack behind and taking the pickax with me, I wade back into the water and start swimming when it gets deep enough. My legs have to do the work, thrusting me forward while my hands grip the pickax. I keep hitting the rocky sides of the shaft. Then I'm in the tightest part, the squeeze, where I can't swim but only crawl. Not enough room to turn around—no choice but to keep going. The first time when it was dry was bad enough, but now underwater pushing myself through like a worm, banging my head and scraping my knees and elbows, I'm gripped with fright so strong it blows my fuses. I panic, thrash around, try to scream, but fear blocks my throat. I convulse and vomit, and the stuff clogs my regulator so I can't breathe. I see only red and black. *I need air! I'm going to die!*

The watcher, the deep, calm part of me, takes over: *You're not going to die. Take the regulator out of your mouth and shake it clear. Then put it back in your mouth and blow through it.*

I do this. It works. I can breathe again. My convulsions become tremors, then fade. I crawl forward, throat and nose burning from stomach acid.

The shaft expands, the water level drops. I can breathe without the regulator and see without the mask. Then I can stand up and walk. It's awkward with the fins, though, so I take them off. I should've brought my shoes, tied them to the belt. The wetsuit socks aren't much protection against the rocks.

I mince down the final slope to where the cavern opens out and the underground ocean stretches before me, calm and still, except for ripples from drops falling from the shiny ceiling. It's as if I've reached the unified field, that quiet expanse that encompasses everything. Now I get to transcend, go into it. I put my fins back on and slip into the water, open my mouth to it, drink the delicious elixir.

I take a good look back at the opening of the vent shaft so I can find it later. I pull the mask down and sink along the wall of the cavern, bubbles streaming up. To go deeper, I release air from my BC. Although the water is clear, the lamp doesn't shine very far, so I have to stay close to the wall, which means I can't see much area as I look for openings—a flooded vent shaft running back towards the earth's surface, so the water will run out from its own pressure when I dig through to the air.

The cavern wall, though, starts to slant in towards the mountain, away from the earth's surface. Rather than following the slant deeper, I stay at this depth and move along the side. Using my legs together in a dolphin kick, I swim a long ways but don't see any openings, just solid rock. I still have an hour of air, but I need to leave enough time to dig and to get back. If I can't find another vent shaft, or if I do but can't dig out to the surface, I'll at least have done what I could. We'll have to accept an honorable defeat.

I come to an underwater cliff where the wall suddenly drops deeper instead of slanting away. Following it down, I find a few small openings running back into the earth. They could be vent shafts, but they're much too small to enter.

I'm getting more worried the plan's not going to work. I'm also getting tired, breath rasping in the regulator, legs like logs. But it's wonderful being here. The water feels more lively than the ocean, despite being very still. No fish or anything, just endless water.

As I go deeper, the cliff slants again and becomes almost flat, what seems to be the bottom. But it could be just a plateau. Whatever it is, it has no shafts.

The time is going. Looks like I've failed. I think of Jane's face as I tell her. She'd understand and would be glad to see me, but she'd still be disappointed to lose the water to Chevron. So would I.

The water here is noticeably warmer. I must be close to the volcanic core, the furnace still burning deep inside Mt. Shasta. I can feel the heat through my wetsuit.

Maybe...what if...might be even more dangerous...but might be worth a try in the time I have left.

I follow the heat, running my hand along the rocks as they get warmer until I find a place where the rocks are actually hot. If I can bring the water in contact with the core, it would boil. But since there's so much water, it would take awhile—long enough for me to get out...probably. As it boiled, it would rise, and when it filled the space, pressure would send it gushing out the shaft. The water would keep boiling and gushing out, because the volcano draws its heat from the center of the earth. Plenty of heat and plenty of water.

I have to try it!

I strike the pickax between the rocks and pry them apart, strike again into the gap between them, pry some more and clear away the hot rubble with my hands, uncover hotter rocks, sweating in my wetsuit as I dig farther. I'm in a hole up to my waist, can feel the heat through my fins. I'm now willing to die, if that's the only way to free the water.

A faint glow comes up from the rocks below. I strike towards it, shoveling broken rocks away with the flat side of the pickax. More hacking blows take me deeper. Heat shimmers are rising through the water. It's getting too hot to stay. One more blow and a prying wrench open a channel to the core. Heat gushes over me. I drop the pickax and flee. I drop my weight belt to ascend faster—I'd rather have the bends than boil to death. The heat follows me up.

By the time I reach the surface, steam is rising from it. I've never been so hot in my life. The air is barely breathable, it's so steamy. There's the opening to my shaft—far away. I shed my tanks for speed and swim towards it like an Olympic sprinter. The water level is rising as it gets hotter. Deep down it must be boiling now—bubbles are streaming up. The temperature increases even more—I feel like I'm being poached in my wetsuit.

I reach the shaft and climb out of the water as the surface begins to seethe and roil. I toss my fins away and clamber up the slope. The water is rising more rapidly, following me. Looking back, I see the other side has broken into a gurgling, rolling boil. Steam burns my nose, throat, and lungs, and I can barely see. I'm worried the lamp will short out from all the moisture. The rising water is up to my ankles, burning my feet.

The shaft gets narrower and turns down towards the flooded section. Water is running down the slope faster than I can; it reaches the flooded section and pools up there. By the time I get there, the water coming from behind is up to my knees. The pain of the heat is almost paralyzing.

I plunge into the flooded section, holding my breath. At first it's hot, then warm, and finally cool, a refreshing delight to my seared skin. It won't take long, though, before this too is boiling. My wetsuit rips on rocks as I force myself through the squeeze. I emerge on the other side, gasping for air. Water has already risen to my pack. I leave it—slow me down too much. I run in a half crouch up the shaft, hearing furious rumbling as the pressure builds up behind the flooded section. If I'm still underground when it breaks through, I'm dead. Hot water is already at my heels, then over my legs.

Finally the shaft opens up, and I can stand. The water is gushing out, but since it has more room to expand here, it drops below my knees. I see the chamber ahead, the hole I dug in the roof, an oval of moonlight wavering and shimmering on the water as the chamber floods. The pressure must be greater now because water is jetting out of the shaft. It rises over my legs again, this time even hotter.

I grab the rope and pull it to make sure it's firm. "Jane!" The loops of rope hurt my feet, but I don't mind. I'm climbing Jacob's Ladder out of hell into heaven. The water is climbing too, but slower than I am.

Jane's face fills the hole. "Bless you, you're alive!" She reaches an arm to help me up. I grab her hand and raise my head up into the summer night—moon, stars, Shasta's shining peak. *Yes—I'm alive!*

I heave myself up onto the ground. Jane hugs me and kisses me on my wetsuited cheek. "I heard these terrible noises," she said. "I thought you were dead."

"We both will be if we don't get out of here!"

As we're backing away, a plume of steam lofts out of the hole, followed by a froth of water that becomes a bubbling fountain, probably mixed with cockroaches, centipedes, and bat shit into a subterranean soup. Soon it's gushing like an open fire hydrant, then it spouts higher, higher yet. Some turns to steam in the cool night air, and the wind blows it into drifting veils and floating trains.

We're retreating, but it's too beautiful not to watch. We walk a few steps forward, then turn around to look again. It's a geyser now shooting straight up 100 feet into the air. The water falling back to earth covers Chevron's drilling equipment and forms a stream running down the slope.

A loud, steady rumble is sounding deep in the mountain. It doesn't get louder, and the geyser doesn't get higher. Both seem to be stable, for now at least. The stream, however, is growing steadily as more and more water jets out. A cloud of steam swells and billows into the starry purple night.

As we walk, I tell Jane about it. Actually I'm more hobbling than walking. My neoprene socks are in tatters, the rocks are digging into my feet. We pause often to rest and look back at the white geyser shining in the moonlight, pumped from the core of the mountain, returning the water to the land.

By the time we reach the motor home I'm leaving blood on the rocks. But more important—the geyser is still leaving water on the rocks, a river coursing with its own inner genius down the line of gravity. The moon is hidden by clouds.

I shower off the grime and blood, and Jane bandages my feet and rubs aloe vera on my pink, parboiled legs. We sleep.

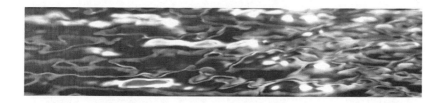

A rustling noise wakes me. Sounds like a fire—where is it? I listen closer. It's many little sounds coming together into a rustle. The little sounds are plinks and plunks and blops and bings. Right above me...on the roof. Rain! The windows are smeared with running water. The air smells different—damp.

I laugh out loud and sit up, but the movement rouses my pain, and I sink back down. My feet are aching and throbbing. They've bled through the bandages and left red smears on the sheets. I hope not on the couch.

I limp into the bathroom and clean up. When I come out, Jane is there already dressed. She beams me a smile. "You did it! The geyser's still spouting, and it's been raining for an hour. You're the hero!" She winces, though, when she sees me limping. "Hurts bad?"

"Yeah. And I ruined your sheets." I show her the bloody splotches.

"We can wash the sheets," she says. "But let me put some fresh bandages on those feet." She leaves and comes back with a bunch of stuff. Sitting beside me on the fold-out couch, she peels off the bandages—hurts, *hurts*, HURTS! With a hesitant, almost fearful expression on her face, she tenderly wipes both feet with a wet washcloth—hurts some more—and dries them with a towel. "No infection, at least not yet. And nothing so deep that it needs to be stitched up." She rubs salve over the cuts and covers them with fresh dressings. Then lotion on the still-red legs. The touch of her hands and the caring expression on her face make me want her. *Forget that,* I tell myself.

Maybe she picked up on my thoughts because she starts

chattering nervously. "I hope you feel the pain was worth it. You succeeded superbly."

"Definitely worth it," I say. "The pain will go away."

"You want to see the geyser?"

"Sure!"

She brings a pair of binoculars, and I kneel on the couch in front of the window. I have to peer through the drops and smears on the glass, but I can see Shasta. As I focus and scan the lower slopes, I see two helicopters buzzing around. Beneath them, a small white line stands out against the dark rocks. It doesn't look like much from here, but as I think of the water jetting out of that boiling cauldron within the mountain, and the immense span of the underground sea, an aquifer stretching hundreds of miles, and the massive heat of the volcanic core, Shasta's hot heart, I know the water will continue to flow, the rains will fall, the drought it over, the earth will be green again. All that would've been worth dying for, but to be alive to enjoy it is much better.

"You rest here," Jane says, "and I'll bring you breakfast."

"OK, thanks."

She comes back in a few minutes with a tray that she sets on the coffee table. "You can stay there," she says, "and I'll give you the food."

At first I think, *I'm not an invalid.* But then I imagine how the floor will feel on my feet, and I stay here.

She sits on the edge of the bed and hands me a cup of coffee. I take a sip and set it on the flat arm of the couch. She holds a bowl of granola, chopped apples, and yogurt, dips a spoon in it, and directs it towards my mouth. My hands don't hurt much, but if this is the way she wants to do it, that's fine. I take the bite and crunch it down. She's wearing a wide necked T-shirt, light blue that looks good with her long gray hair cascading like water over her shoulders and down her back. Around her neck and disappearing into the T-shirt is a strand of coral beads. I don't know why she doesn't wear it on the outside, and I can't help wondering what else she has in there.

"Let me give you a muffin," she says and reaches a mound of whole wheat and chocolate chips to me. I take it with one hand and hold her hand with the other, lean toward her and see her green eyes widen as I kiss her on the lips. Before she can resist, I draw her closer and kiss her again, this time longer.

She gasps when I pull my lips away. Her eyes are closed. I hold her face in both my hands and kiss her lingeringly. She doesn't kiss back but doesn't move away. Then she opens her eyes, looking frightened. "Bob, no, we can't."

"Yes, we can. You said I was the hero. And the hero gets the girl. And you're the girl! Those are the rules."

"But—"

I kiss her again to keep her quiet, brush my tongue against her lips. They part just a bit. "No-o-o," she says but it's more of a sigh. It parts her lips enough for my tongue to slip in. Mine seeks hers, which flees at first touch but finds there's no place to hide so stays put and allows itself to be petted, even tussles back a bit. I stroke her streaming hair, her neck, her back. She's returning my kisses now with shy little nibbles.

I rub my chest against hers, and she reflexively rubs back but gives a self-disapproving sob at her surrender. I touch her breasts, rubbing and fondling them, and she inhales sharply and closes her eyes tighter. She's small in my arms. I can rub and pat her all over now. I uncover her, and she turns her face away. Her body is wrinkled but very lovely. Her breasts sag but still have a lush fullness to them, and the nipples are pert and prickled with excitement. When I kiss and suck them, she presses my head to her chest. After a blissful while I move up to her lips, open and yielding now, and her tongue greets mine.

As we gaze into each other's eyes, it's clear: I love her and she loves me and we have to do this.

"I may be very dry," she says. "Use the lotion."

Instead I use my tongue, licking her dear cleft, pink, bright, and lively as any eighteen-year-old's. As I suck her swollen node, her tummy and hips quiver and she makes little sounds that get faster and louder until she arches off the bed with a shout of joy. She thrashes convulsively over the mattress and knocks the coffee off the arm of the couch. It crashes to the floor. "Leave it," she moans. "I'll get it later."

She's lying there, hips raised, hair streaming, looking young, wild, and utterly gorgeous. "Put it in me!"

As I do, I'm so overwhelmed with love for her that I start to cry. It's unfair to have so little time together. Seeing my tears, she understands and hers flow too. We hold each other, arms and legs wrapped tightly around, fusing into one being for as long as we're together. Time. This is our time. Treasure it while we have it.

We peak together in a glory of writhing bodies, kissing and crying and murmuring our love. She clings to me from underneath, and I pick her up and rock her in my arms. Clasped in liquid embrace, we nestle in afterglow, astounded by this power. We can't talk, all we can do is hold each other. And we do that long and lovingly, cuddling in a puddle of our wetness.

She languidly says, "We can go home now. We've finished our work here." Her hands caress me. "But you're going to need some shoes. I hope the windshield wipers work. I've never used them before."

They do. She drives into Weed and we find a shoe store. My feet are too swollen for regular shoes, so I get rubber thongs and a pair of air-cushioned joggers for later. We buy more bandages. We try to buy umbrellas, but they're sold out.

We drive back to the mountain to get a closer look. The road is flooded, a 100-foot swath of water coursing across it from the forest on one side and back into forest on the other. The grass and bushes along its edges seem already greener. The geyser is still jetting straight up where Shasta starts to rise. The rain falls lightly but steadily.

A crowd of happily amazed people are milling around the bank of the river, some with umbrellas and raincoats, some with sheets of plastic over their heads, others just wet. Laughing children run around trying to catch raindrops on their tongues. Water is dripping off my nose and off Jane's sun hat. Her T-shirt is wet, nipples standing out. I can't wait to kiss them again.

We walk around holding hands, hearing snippets of conversation: "Have to build a bridge." "No problem, the New River Bridge. Put it right here." "The water's already filling the dry Sacramento River. Keeps up, it'll get to the whole Central Valley." "President just declared it the Shasta Geyser National Monument. Now no one can drill." "Nobody knows how it happened—a freak of nature." "We know! It's the Lord's work! He answered our prayers and saved us. The miracle of Mt. Shasta!"

Jane and I get back in the Winnebago. I kiss her on the lips, and we drive home in the rain.

COSMIC
EGG
BOOKS

If you prefer to spend your nights with Vampires and
Werewolves rather than the mundane then we publish the books
for you. If your preference is for Dragons and Faeries or Angels
and Demons – we should be your first stop. Perhaps your
perfect partner has artificial skin or comes from another planet –
step right this way. Our curiosity shop contains treasures you
will enjoy unearthing. If your passion is Fantasy (including
magical realism and spiritual fantasy), Horror or Science Fiction
(including Steampunk), Cosmic Egg books will
feed your hunger.